The Blockwives
of
Atlanta
By
Sevyn McCray

The Block wives of Atlanta
By Sevyn McCray

Acknowledgements

All praise is due to my father in heaven who put this dream in me. Not many people grow up to be what they always wanted to be. To my two beautiful children Christopher Mahlik and Cristany Mahliya, thank you for continuing to be the anchor that has kept me grounded. To my family the Price's, the Gore's & my extended family the Atchisons thank you for your continuous support. I love each and every one of you.

To all of my friends who are closer than my family has been, My first friends…. It's so many of you let me just say C.M. Pitts and the "Stewart Click" that sums it. You know who you are. My Chicas, how can I not mention you all? Cassie Evans, Nisha Fletcher, Kobie Andrews, Nicki Carter, Kiska Lyons, Tracy Towns and my Wednesday Girls Olivia Lewis & Takia Jones, I love you girls and thanks for always being there and listening #MyWholeTeamWinning. The entire Zone 1 #30318 until the death of me, I have to represent for us. I can't forget about Adamsville/Flatland, thanks for friendships and the lessons. Fifth ward and Zone 3 welcomed me like I was one of their own, much love from Joyland to Summer Hill to Jonesboro Road and everything in between.

David Weaver, talk about always on time. I appreciate every thing, it is too much to list, thank you and much love. My Aquarius sister and "Literary Consultant" Sam Johnson-Bonsu girl what can I say? You have been here since the beginning of the ride, trained and ready to go. You are my "Write hand" Words cannot convey the love I have for you doll. You just don't know how much that has meant to me. To all my other author friends that I have made on Facebook I love each and every one of you. A special shout out to my pudd Allison

Grace (the know-it-all.) All of my sisters and brothers in lit on the Bankroll Squad who welcomed me right on into the fold.

Brittani Williams, my graphic artist. I told you my idea and sent you a few pictures and as always you delivered in record timing.

My brothers from another that helped me through this, Quinton, Toe-Toe and Nard Chico. I got nothing but love for you! Slimm babe, I did it again! If I forgot anyone charge it to my head not my heart.... I got you on the next go round! But if you are one of my Facebook fam, twitter or Instagram followers consider yourself counted in!!!! Special shout out to April Showers and Shay Moore you two ladies blogged about "Da Lick" and gave me great exposure. Love yall. And last but not least my brothers Santos/Dino "Big Puncho" Price and Randy R.J. Menefee…. Ya'll made me thorough!

Follow me on Twitter at @I_amSevyn or check me out on Facebook Sevyn McCray (the Author) or www.sevynmccray.com . I love you all x10. Bankroll Squad is not just a name…... It's a lifestyle! #SquardUp #TBRS

Prologue

Chrissy sat in the courtroom confidently. She knew they had the best legal team in the south and Whyte was finally coming home to her. Not having him home this year had been killing her slowly. As the judge came out of her private quarters, she stood and held her head up high. This nightmare was finally about to be over. She glanced at her three friends, who she had met at the beginning of this ordeal, they were now closer to her than her own sister. They reassured her with smiles. Chrissy returned her focus to the front of the courtroom and looked at the back of her husband's head; she knew he felt her presence. The bailiff called the courtroom to order and Whyte's lawyer stood up.

Chrissy sat back down and Tameka reached over and grabbed her hand. She knew Chrissy was a ball of nerves. Tameka felt Chrissy's hand perspiring and her heart racing. They were expected to come down on Whyte much harder because he was the ringleader of it all. Her husband's trial was set to start next week. He had been reassuring her that everything was going to be alright and they would all be coming home soon. She remembered the last conversation she had with her husband when she went to visit him at the federal holding facility in Lovejoy, Georgia.

"Baby, don't worry. We're gonna bounce back from this. Just stay prayed up. I'm making some moves in here. I just need you to be on stand-by. When I tell you to move, you move. I'mma need you on the outside making the literal moves. Jordyn got out after being locked up for only a month because they had bullshit on her. All of us are gonna walk out on top; we have the best attorneys. Be patient and prayerful." Tameka believed every word her husband said; she was simply waiting for the event that he spoke of to unfold. She had been doing her best to keep the spirits of the other girls lifted.

They were a united front. A year ago, they were all virtually strangers. However, after the indictment came down against Whyte and his affiliates, they were thrown together. Now they knew each others secrets, feelings, and thoughts.

She sat there in her own world, daydreaming about the last time they were together. Chaney had held onto a secret for a longtime. Even so, she knew it would eventually come to light. They had shared so many good times together. He had shown her how it felt to be a real woman. She had fallen in love with him and he had never even touched her. He had restored her confidence in herself. And for that, she would forever be indebted to him. Even though she wanted him for herself, she knew that could never happen because Whyte loved his wife.

Chaney continued to think of all she had endured in the last two years. She went from being hopelessly in love with her husband to not even wanting to see his face. For as long as she could, she put up a front. However, once the truth surfaced about Dude, there was no turning back. The lie they had been living was out for everyone to see. She wanted to move away; she couldn't stand people looking at her as though she was a monster when she hadn't done anything wrong. Perhaps, the fact that she went along with the lie was just as bad as being the liar.

When she heard Chrissy scream, she was startled out of her daydream. Chaney looked over to see that her friend had passed out. She glanced to the front of the courtroom just in time to witness the bailiff grab Whyte as he launched toward his attorney.

He hollered. "I thought you said you could pull this off. I paid you over a hundred thousand dollars–a hundred thousand dollars, and I still got ten years!"

Chapter 1: One Plus One Equals Happy

"Baby, I don't know why you can't postpone this until I get back. You don't need to have any plastic surgery; you're perfect to me. I'll tell you what, call your doctor and see if he can postpone it until next Monday." Whyte sat at the island in their massive kitchen and ate the banana nut oat pancakes that he loved.

Chrissy had to be at the hospital for her surgery in an hour, but she still made sure to get up and fix his favorite meal before he left. Whyte was due in New York for a big meeting this morning. Because his connect, Ponchees was flying in from Mexico, it couldn't be postponed. Even so, Chrissy refused to postpone her surgery.

"Daviyd don't act like that; I'm going to be okay. Pretty is going to be with me every step of the way. Quit worrying. My health is A-1 now. When I had my pre-op appointment, my blood pressure was fine and my blood sugar has been level for the entire year. I can't help that something came up with you. I've been planning this surgery for almost a year. When you come home, I'm going to be a new person." Chrissy went over and planted a kiss on Whyte's forehead as he continued to eat, then she walked up the back stairs to their bedroom.

He knew he couldn't postpone this meeting. Ponchees had not been in the states in over nine months. Therefore, if he wanted to meet up with him, he was going to have to go to New York. Whyte really wished that Chrissy wasn't going through with this plastic surgery mess. Ever since she had the lap band weight loss surgery two years ago and had lost over one hundred pounds, she was so self-conscious about how she looked with or without clothes. He had given her the money for her birthday to have everything done, but he didn't think she would go through with it. Now Chrissy was about to have a body lift–the extra skin removed from her arms and a breast lift. This was one time he wished he had told her no when she requested the money. However, it wouldn't have made a difference 'because Chrissy had her own money.

Christyn, better known as Chrissy, rushed around their master suite making sure that Whyte had everything he needed for his trip to New York. She wasn't worried about herself or what she needed for her overnight hospital stay. Her best friend and assistant Pretty had packed her bag last week. It was funny, Pretty took care of Chrissy and Chrissy took care of Whyte. After checking his Louis Vuitton duffle bag one last time, she closed it. He had told her that he just needed the necessities. While there, he planned to take a day and go shopping, and bring them some exclusive items back. Chrissy walked through an adjacent bedroom, which was considered to be Whyte's bedroom, went into his closet, retrieved something for him to wear, and laid it across the bed. Because he did big and small things for her and had been doing it for eight years now, she took pride in doing little things for him.

Whyte snuck up behind her as she was putting the last of his underwear inside the duffle bag. Moving her hair from her neck, he gently planted kisses along her hairline. Chrissy moaned slightly as he took her earlobe into his mouth and sucked on it. She was getting hot. "Stop bae, you know that's my spot." She murmured as her breathing became shallow.

"I know it is." Whyte turned Chrissy around to face him and kissed her passionately as he put his hands under her satin nightshirt. Their tongues danced in each other's mouth as Chrissy grabbed handfuls of his hair and returned his kisses with fervor.

"What time is your flight?" Chrissy had began to unbutton her husband's jeans as he was lifting her shirt over her head.

"I have time. If not, I'll make time because when I come home, you'll be recovering. You'll be so sore, you won't be able to stand my touch. Do you think you can go that long without some of this?" He gripped his penis through his Ralph Lauren boxer briefs.

"That's why I need to get it really good right now." Chrissy said breathlessly as she stood before her husband naked.

Whyte cupped both of her breasts in his hands as he alternated between them– kissing, sucking, and licking.

Chrissy moaned and said "baby just think, when you get back, there will be a new me.

She remembered meeting him at the green store on Northside Drive when she was sixteen years old. That day changed her life forever. Chrissy was never the same. She was standing at the counter buying some swisher sweet blunts. "You are too pretty to be doing something so ugly." She remembered him saying. His deep voice sent chills down her spine. Chrissy turned around and the tall, light-skinned man was standing in line behind her with a bag of dill pickle chips and an oatmeal pie. She looked up at him; he had to be at least 6'4" because she was 5'10" herself. His eyes were the color of the ocean and his hair was dark blonde. He actually looked like a white man with a dark tan.

Chrissy was so self-conscious that she wanted to leave the box of blunts right there. "If you lived in my house, you'd be smoking more than a blunt." She told him. Grabbing the box and walking out of the door, she put the swishers in the back pocket of her Baby Phat jeans and walked down the block. She was lucky that her best friend was the neighborhood weed man. Therefore, she never paid for it. All she had to do was come prepared with blunt papers and roll on command. D-Rock supplied her all of the weed she wanted to smoke.

The chocolate girl with the big doe eyes and squeaky voice enchanted Whyte. He could see the pain in them; he wanted to know more. What was going on at her home that made her defile her beauty and femininity by smoking weed? He jumped in his Yukon and followed her as she walked down the block. Creeping at a turtle's pace, when he got beside her, he lowered his window and turned his music down. "Can I give you a ride somewhere?"

Chrissy's mind was still on the tall, light-skinned man as she walked up the block. She was on her way to pick up her book bag which she had dropped on her porch. She hadn't gone in the house yet, and didn't plan on going in until it was time to go to sleep. Her mother didn't care if she never came home. All she ever worried about was her younger sister, Dior. Chrissy was so happy she was graduating a year early. She was going to take the first offer she received from an out-of-town college, and get the hell away from her evil momma and sister, as well as her weak father. A truck pulled up beside her, rolled the window down, and there he was. He asked if he could give her a ride, but she shook her head and continued walking toward her house. The guy didn't pull off as she expected. Instead, he drove slowly as she reached her porch, picked up her book bag, and continued up the block. Just as Chrissy was about to cross the street, the light turned red. He leaned over and asked her again, did she want a ride. She turned and looked at him; she could tell he was older but like a moth to a flame, she was drawn to him. This time she said yes. She walked around the back of the truck and opened the door. As she sat down, he reached over and grabbed the pistol off the seat. She tried her hardest not to smile. Yet, as soon as she closed the truck door, something on the inside felt so right to her.

"So, where am I taking you?" Whyte asked the young lady who hunched her shoulders. "What do you mean you don't know? Where were you walking to? I can drop you off. Oh, by the way, my name is Whyte. What's yours?" He reached over and extended one hand as he kept the other one on the steering wheel.

"I'm Chrissy. I don't have anywhere to go; I just know I don't wanna go home. I was headed to my homeboy's house." She looked at him as he drove pass where Dee Rock lived. She didn't stop him; she could see Dee Rock anytime; she wanted to kick-it with Whyte. "Can I ask you a question?"

"Yeah, lil' buddy, go ahead." He replied as he kept his eyes on the road. He probably should have at least felt some type of apprehension as a result of having a girl in the car that he didn't know. But he didn't. Actually, he felt at ease.

"Are you white or black?" I mean, you look white but you sound black. I don't mean to offend you, but what's your ethnicity?"

"Baby, it depends on who you ask." Whyte said, laughing to himself.

"I guess that means you're not gonna answer the question. Where are you from then?" Chrissy wanted to start some type of dialogue with Whyte; she wasn't ready for him to drop her off yet.

"I'm from a lil' bit of everywhere baby." Whyte liked the way she was looking at him sideways as he drove toward Pittsburgh.

"Are you taking me with you?" She looked out of the dark, tinted window and noticed they were no longer on the Westside.

"You said you didn't have anywhere to go, and didn't want to go home. Well, I have a basketball game to be at in twenty minutes. So, I'm taking you with me.

"Really, are we going to see the Hawks play?" Chrissy was excited; she had just met him and he was taking her to a pro basketball game already.

"Naw, baby girl. I have my own team and we play at the recreation center on Tuesday and Thursday evenings."

She was a little disappointed, but didn't let on. "Oh really, that's cool. I needed to get out of the hood anyway."

They pulled up at the recreation center in the Pittsburgh community. All the fly rides were parked in the parking lot. People were walking in and dressed like they were going to a professional basketball game. Whyte hopped out, opened his hatch, removed a Nike gym bag, and then opened the door for Chrissy.

Chrissy saw the large crowd and once again, had feelings of insecurity. She still had on the Baby Phat outfit that she'd worn to school with a pair of Nike Air Force 1s. She exited the truck and looked around as several people rushed up to Whyte like he was a superstar. He was politicking–providing daps, kissing babies, and giving out hugs. When the ice cream truck pulled into the parking lot, a little boy, whom he had just hugged, asked him to buy him an ice cream. He grabbed Chrissy's hand as she stood there. "Here, take this to the ice cream man and tell him I said give the kids whatever they want until it runs out." He had reached into his pocket, pulled out a wad of money, and peeled off three crisp one hundred dollar bills. She did as she was told. Once they'd gotten word that Whyte had bought it out, all the children ran to the truck. As he stood there and kicked it with his homeboys, one-by-one, the children approached him eating ice cream, pickles, chips and soda, and thanked him continuously. He replied, "no problem, anytime."

Whyte saw that everyone had come out to watch the Pittsburgh versus Mechanicville game. He knew major bets would be placed. Glancing down at his Rolex, he saw it was time for him to start getting ready. Grasping Chrissy's hand, they walked toward the gym. He heard all the whispers but didn't say anything; he just hoped she didn't feel a certain type of way or pay attention to the people. When they got inside and he was about to enter the locker room to change clothes, he removed his diamond-encrusted chain that had a huge Star of David on it, and put it around her neck. Then he took off his Rolex and asked her to put it away. Seeing the uncertainty in her eyes, he lifted the necklace by the charm and said, "this means you belong to me. This is my hood. You don't have to worry about a thing. Sit on that side." He pointed to the side that everyone from Pittsburgh was sitting on, and then disappeared through the double doors.

Chapter 2: More Than A Little Freaky

Chaney had just left the office, she was mentally fatigued. Every time she turned around, Dude was going out-of-town on a business trip to meet with a major label. She understood that he was passionate about his record label but felt there was much more to it. She came in the front door and kicked her heels off in the foyer. Looking around her house as she walked through it, she calmed down once she realized Dude was doing all of this for them. He was taking his dirty money and making it clean. Chaney entered the den and went to the bar area. She poured one shot of Patron and a glass of Moscato, then took them both upstairs.

She had to admit, she appreciated the times when she was alone. However, it seemed she was always by herself these days. Chaney removed her clothes and looked in the dresser mirror at her perfect body. She didn't have an ounce of fat or a stretch mark anywhere. After she had her last miscarriage, she had gone on a diet for three months, then went and had liposuction. Now, her body was in the same shape that it was four years ago when she first met Dude while working at Onyx.

Her life changed that night. Regrettably, from where she was sitting, she couldn't tell if it had changed for the better or worse. As she took the patron shot straight to the head, thinking of all that she was going through brought tears to her eyes.

Chaney went into the master bath and turned on the water. Maybe a hot bubble bath along with the drinks would relax her. This weekend, she decided she would make an appointment to go to Spa Essential Essence for the full treatment. With all the shit she puts up with, she deserved the luxury. She decided to listen to Adele's 21 album in her bathroom, then her phone rang. Although it was an unknown number, she decided to answer it anyway. Dude was out-of-town; it could have been him calling from his hotel.

"You at home all by yourself and your husband is in L.A. walking down Rodeo drive holding hands with another nigga. Bitch, you're dumber than you look." Chaney didn't recognize the voice and the number was blocked. Therefore, she placed her phone on the counter, went to the medicine cabinet, and took out an Ambien sleeping pill. She was going to take it as soon as she got out of the tub; she needed sleep and needed it fast. The phone rang again, she saw that it was another unknown call. This time, she didn't answer; she simply powered her phone off, got in the king size garden tub, and allowed Adele to serenade her.

More than an hour had passed, and the water was freezing cold. The combination of alcohol and exhaustion had knocked Chaney out. She probably would have stayed asleep in the tub if the cold ass water had not wakened her. She jumped out of the tub and ran across her bathroom to get her bathrobe. She slipped into the robe and her slippers, grabbed her phone from the counter, and went downstairs to her kitchen. She hadn't eaten all day. Knowing there wasn't anything in the refrigerator because she couldn't remember the last time she'd been grocery shopping. Chaney did find some frozen lasagna in the freezer and popped it into the microwave. After powering her phone on to check her messages, it immediately began to ring. It was the unknown number again. This time, she decided to answer and say something to the person. "Who is this? What do you want?"

"What is it gonna take for you to wake up? That nigga is fucking punks and probably getting fucked and you're not gon' realize the truth until it's too late. Are you gonna wait until you're somewhere dying a slow death because you love his down-low ass. Don't let that fake thug shit fool you." The person hung up. The voice was unrecognizable, something had been used to disguise it.

Chaney's appetite had been spoiled. She left the lasagna in the microwave, and went into the den to fix herself another drink. Instead of pouring another glass of Moscato, she decided to take the entire bottle back to her bedroom. With a million thoughts going through her head, she climbed the steps. She wasn't angry at the caller who was disrupting her life; she was mad at herself because all the signs had been there. She shrugged it off, but deep down inside, she knew what it was. Chaney never shared with anyone the things she and Dude did behind closed doors. She was freaky, but he was a lil' too freaky.

The first night she met him, she went home with him. She remembered him grabbing her arm when she first walked onto the floor. Chaney danced for him the entire night. He didn't try to touch her; he kept her drinks coming and tipped her well. When the lights came on, and as the club was closing, she was about to walk away when he gave her a one hundred dollar tip and asked if she would have breakfast with him. Dude seemed sweet enough, so she told him yes she would eat with him. She recalled he wasn't flashy. Yet, he looked like money. His dreads were neatly twisted into two french braids and he wore a Yankees hat. He had on a pair of Seven for all Mankind jeans, some Bally tennis shoes with the matching belt, and a nice platinum cross that was filled with diamonds and hung all the way down to his stomach. But his Presidential Rolex commanded attention.

Chaney freshened up and slipped into a Nike bodysuit with matching Air Max and pulled her hair into a ponytail. She grabbed her duffle bag and walked out the door. She didn't see Dude anywhere. Therefore, she headed toward her black Mercedes CLK and hopped in, throwing her bag in the back. Just as she was pulling out of the parking lot, a black H2 Hummer pulled in front of her, blocking her from exiting the parking lot. The dark tint prevented Chaney from seeing inside. She laid on her horn so they would move. The window rolled down. Dude leaned over and shouted "follow me." Chaney turned up

Lil Wayne's The Carter 2 CD and jumped on the highway following Dude. She had no idea where they were going and didn't have his number, so she vibed to Lil Wayne as he played through her speakers. Zipping in and out of traffic, she continued to follow him.

Getting off the highway at the West Peachtree Street exit, she was right behind him as he turned into the Twelve Building at 400 West Peachtree. Chaney knew the building had restaurants in it, but none of them were open this time of night. She parked beside him in the parking deck. He jumped out of his truck and rushed to open her car door for her.

"They have a breakfast spot in here?" Chaney asked Dude as she exited the car and locked her doors with the key fob.

"Yes ma'am, and it has the best view of the city. It's on the top floor and the cook can really burn. I know you're going to love his skills." They got on the elevator and he pressed P for the penthouse floor.

Chaney looked around as they stepped off the elevator. There were only two doors on the entire floor and no sign of a restaurant. Apprehensively, she followed Dude as he went to one of the doors and used a key to enter. He opened the door and she stood to the side. "I don't know who you think I am, or what you have planned, but it's four thirty in the morning and I didn't plan on coming to your place. I thought we were going to breakfast. Maybe you need to try one of them other girls at the club 'cause I don't care how many ones you threw at me tonight, you didn't purchase me. Plus, I don't sell pussy." She turned around and walked back toward the elevator.

Dude followed behind Chaney as she walked down the hall. When she pressed the elevator button, he put his hand on top of hers, attempting to stop her from pushing the button. "Lil' mama, I didn't mean any harm. I'm really big on vibes. I got a good vibe from you. I come in Onyx all the time. If I wanted to buy pussy, trust me I know who's selling it in there. Come back and enjoy breakfast. I just went grocery shopping; I can cook you whatever you want."

She looked at him sideways as the elevator doors opened. He pulled a pistol from his waistband; she screamed and jumped on the elevator. Frantically, Chaney pushed the elevator button. However, the doors wouldn't close because he had his other hand holding it open. "Please don't hurt me! I left my money in my car. I don't have anything but my jewelry; you can have it." She began twisting her rings off of her fingers one at a time.

"Wait-a-minute, wait-a-minute! Damn, lil' momma. What type of niggas you use to fucking with? I ain't 'bout to rob or rape you. I was trying to give you my gun, so you would feel safe. If I make a false move, you shoot." Dude could see the panic in her eyes as they had doubled in size. She was truly frightened.

Chaney looked at the gun in his palm that he was extending to her, then stared into his eyes. She saw sincerity in them, not malice. Either this nigga was a good actor, or he actually meant every word he said. She stepped off of the elevator, allowing it to close behind her. That began the first of many mornings of her eating breakfast with him after her work-shift was over.

Chapter 3: I'm a Hustler Baby!

Jordyn sat on the sofa and puffed on the kush blunt. She was tired as hell; she had been up hustling all night long. She leaned forward and put another stack of money in the money counter. All she wanted to do was go home, get into bed with her two children, and enjoy them for once. Dent's sorry ass didn't hustle and he didn't want to spend any time with the kids. His only interests were spending money, living life as Whyte's shadow, and smoking weed. Jordyn knew she could do better, but the thought of starting over with someone else was extremely frightening.

She put the blunt out, got up to get some more rubber bands and retrieve the duffle bag from the back room. She was waiting on her little brother, Noah, also known as Lucky, to pull up so that he could take over the dayshift. When she called home, her little sister, Destiny had informed her that Dent hadn't come home. It was time for her to take her sister to majorette practice. Jordyn stuffed all of the stacks of money, totaling thirty-seven thousand dollars, inside a MCM duffle bag, and placed the money counter in the hall closet.

Jordyn heard the keys turning in the burglar bar door. Even though she knew her brother was the only one that had a key, she still reached for her nine-millimeter pistol. Lucky came in the door smiling with a bag of food and a blunt in his mouth. He was his sister's backbone.

"Damn sis, you look like you've been up all night. The spot was bunking, huh? They didn't give you a chance to sleep." Lucky tried to help his sister as much he could since he had been back home from college. The bags under her eyes were more prominent than usual against her light skin. He opened the bag and handed her a Styrofoam container. "Just some tilapia and grits, I stopped at Unity on my way here."

"'Preciate it Luck. I have to hurry. I have to pick up Destiny and take her to some twirling camp that I paid an arm and a leg for. You have some money on you? 'Cause I have all the money right here and you might need a lil' something for change when the customers start to roll in. I'll call you later. I'm about to go home, get a few hours of rest, and then I'm taking the kids somewhere today. They deserve it. I trap all the time and their daddy ain't hitting on shit. They shouldn't suffer the consequences of both of us being in the streets." Jordyn planned to look online and find something that Peace and Joi could do today. Even though they were only five and six, they could tell when something wasn't right with her and Dent. Even Ray Charles could see that.

When Jordyn pulled into the gates of Niskey Lake Falls, she got a little emotional. Two years ago, she was living in a two-bedroom, one-bath apartment in Flipper Temple with her lights about to be cut off. Her mother had just been found dead in a dope house on Hollywood Road. Due to neglect, her little sister and brother were already staying with her because DFACS had taken them away from her mother six months before. Jordyn and her family were cramped in that two-bedroom apartment. She was sad–depressed; she didn't know where to turn. The state had cremated her mother because there wasn't any money to bury her. Kimberly may not have been the best mother, in fact, she was far from it, but when Jordyn couldn't even afford to have a small funeral for her mother, an internal fire had been unleashed.

She wanted better for her siblings and children. There was a way out of that big black hole; she just had to find it.

That was then–before she found the insurance policy in the rooming house where her mother lived. She had put off going over there because she didn't want to face the pain that it was sure to cause. Nonetheless, after the owner called and informed her she had to remove her mother's belongings or continue to pay rent, equipped with garbage bags, she went. Jordyn's little brother had already returned to school at Savannah State University. He was in his freshman year. Therefore, she was alone when she packed up her mother's stuff. She didn't even go through it, she would do that when she got home. Jordyn filled the three heavy-duty trash bags with all of her mother's things, put them in her 2001 Ford Crown Victoria, and didn't look back. That was the first day of a new beginning.

Later that evening, as she and her little sister, Destiny went through her mother's possessions that were on the living room floor of her apartment, she found a life insurance policy for fifty thousand dollars. To some people, it may not have been much. Then again, everyone wasn't built like Jordyn. She was a natural-born hustler who was determined to increase the capital she had been blessed with.

Two and a half years later, with over five hundred thousand dollars in savings, some investment properties, a mini mansion, and four cars that were paid for, Jordyn was sitting pretty. Her only downfall or mistake was taking Dent back went he got out of jail. Obviously, she didn't need him. By the time he was released, she was doing better than good by herself. She was still trappin' in the trenches most days and being a mother to her two children and younger sister. All Dent did was drop in, play with the kids, eat, fuck her, get some money, and he was back out. He hung around some get-money niggas, but that's all he did–hang around them.

Jordyn thought about her previous life–waking up every morning, putting on a nurse's uniform, and going into stores boosting–all to put a roof over their heads and clothes on their backs. She had come too far, so she decided not to complain.

One of the major reasons she'd put up with Dent and his shit was because she wanted her children to grow up in a two-parent household. Jordyn had never even seen her father. All she knew about him was he was of Italian descent.

Her mother didn't like black men due to the fact that her own father raped her when she was fourteen. Both her sister and brother had Spanish fathers; one was Cuban and the other Puerto Rican.

Dent didn't play a major role in the lives of his children. Truth be told, it was a one-parent household. He was a visitor who happened to have clothes in the closet. Sometimes, Jordyn felt as though she was paying him to stick around and be a father to his kids. Deep in thought, before she knew it, she had pulled up to Welcome All Park recreation center where Destiny's class was being held. She guessed she was on autopilot. Destiny leaned over, gave Jordyn a kiss on the cheek, and told her she would call her. "Wait a minute! Here's a little something so that you'll have money in your pocket." Jordyn handed her sister a crisp fifty-dollar bill, even though she probably already had money.

Peace and Joi were in the backseat of the truck quietly watching a movie. She was so thankful that her genes were dominant. Both of her children were the spitting image of her. Although a year apart, they were the same size, and the only thing that separated them was the fact that they were the opposite sex. Against his father's wishes, Jordyn had recently cut Peace's waist-length braids. When his hair was long, her children looked like identical twins to strangers.

Jordyn was tired; she pulled down the sun visor and looked in the mirror. She had bags under her eyes and her naturally curly hair was all over the place. Nevertheless, before she left the trap house, she had promised herself she would make time for her kids. Jordyn turned around in her seat and noticed that Destiny had already gotten them ready for the day. They had on matching Polo outfits. "Y'all want pancakes?" Their faces lit up like Christmas as they nodded their heads. She figured she could sleep when she was dead. Therefore, they headed north to The Pancake House on Cheshire Bridge Road. She turned on the music and the calming sounds of Corinne Bailey Rae flowed throughout her Q7 Audi truck.

By the time she pulled up at the restaurant, the kids had gotten quiet. It was extremely crowded; she looked back at them and they both had fallen asleep. Pulling out her handicap decal from the glove compartment, she placed it in the window. Jordyn hopped out in front to see how long the wait would be. Although she had been in the trap all night, she still dressed fly at all times. She had on a pair of Robbin's Jeans, a wife beater with a navy blue blazer on top, and a pair of Christian Louboutin high-top sneakers. However, what commanded the most attention was her jewelry. She wore the biggest platinum and diamond-filled cross necklace that was so thin that it looked like the cross was suspended in air. She also had on a bronze colored Gucci sport watch that she had blinged the bezel out on. Her fashion ensemble was completed with earrings that were five carats each. Jordyn looked like money.

The restaurant was filled with people and especially busy. She guessed everyone had the same idea on this sunny Saturday morning. After asking the hostess how long the wait time would be for one adult and two children, she was informed twenty minutes or less. Jordyn provided her name and returned to the truck. She unlocked it, got inside, pulled out her Galaxy Note Tablet, and decided to catch up on some reading which was her passion. She loved reading as well as writing. David Weaver engrossed Jordyn with his "The Lipstick Clique 2" narrative. However, something told her to look up. Dent was walking out of the restaurant, hand-in-hand, with a big butt, blonde-haired girl that looked very familiar. Her first instinct was to pull out her pistol, let down her window, and shoot his ass–that would be another insurance check for her. But she didn't. She pulled out her iPhone 5 and snapped some pictures of them. This was going to come in handy since she knew he would try to lie about it. Jordyn called his phone to see if he would pick up. He didn't. Next, she called Sprint customer service and blocked Dent's number. Finally, she dialed 911 and stated that when she got home her BMW 650 was gone. That'll fix his ass. As of now, his free ride was officially over! When a woman's fed up, there's nothing you can do about it.

Chapter 4: Two Different Lives

After a long day at work, all Tameka wanted to do was go home, but she had gotten a call from her former professor, who she was also sleeping with. She was told to meet at their spot, which happened to be a condo in downtown Atlanta. Tameka felt as if she owed her old professor a big debt. Without her, she wouldn't have finished school at the top of her class, gotten the free ride to law school. or have her job as a paralegal in the eleventh circuit of the U.S. District Court. Albeit, the love affair was long over, Tameka was still at the professor's–who now was a judge–beck and call.

Her husband, Jonathan didn't know they had a sexual relationship. He believed the professor was her mentor and was always there for her if needed. Little did he know, whenever the professor was able to get away from work, meant a stolen moment for them, an opportunity to be in one another's company.

Exhausted beyond belief, Tameka made it to the building off of Tenth Street in record time since rush-hour traffic had died down. She used her pass code to enter the building from the parking deck. When she got out on the fourteenth floor, she used her set of keys to enter the luxurious condo overlooking the city skyline. The living room was filled with candles. The smell was intoxicating. Tameka looked around and didn't see anyone. The dining room table was set, and had a bottle of wine chilling on it. She could smell food. However, didn't see anything cooking. She felt guilty because, once again, the professor had gone all out to make her feel special. Sadly, all she wanted to do was hurry up, fuck, then leave. Actually, she didn't even want to fuck but she knew it was part of her duties.

Coming from the bedroom, dressed in a silk robe, the judge embraced her and kissed her passionately. As soon as their tongues met, a wildfire spread through Tameka. Between her legs began to throb. No matter how much she wanted to walk away from this affair and have an honest relationship with her husband, she had to admit she enjoyed the power, as well as the perks that came with her and the judge's association. While her blouse was being unbuttoned, Tameka tried to remove the silk robe. Like animals, they were tearing into one another. Finally, Tameka managed to get the robe off, bent her head down, put her lips to the judge's breasts, and sucked and teased each nipple while reaching down to massage between the judge's legs. The judge interrupted her and said, "let's go in our room."

As they walked to the bedroom, the robe and all of Tameka's clothes were coming off. It was something about being in control when she was having sex with the judge that made Tameka feel so powerful. She pushed the judge down onto the bed, lay down beside her, and began to kiss her passionately. For five years, Tameka had been in a lesbian relationship with the most powerful judge in the eleventh circuit. Throughout college, she had received a brand new Lexus, the best grades, and a scholarship that not only had the judge's sorority sponsored, but that had paid for her entire law school education. It remained hers, as long as she kept a B average, and a job that every student in her graduating class would have killed for–not to mention the multitude of gifts as well as trips that were supposed to be business. However, most of the time they were pleasure. Tameka had safeguarded Judge Janice Matheson's secret, and fulfilled her fantasy all while she reaped the benefits.

Janice tossed her head back in ecstasy, opened her legs, and started to play with herself. Tameka sucked on her breasts and watched as she tried to bring herself to orgasm. Seeing she was having difficulties, Tameka moved Janice's hand out of the way and worked her magic on Janice who was soaking wet. Janice arched her back as her orgasm took over. She began to shake, then compressed her legs tightly on Tameka's hand. After recuperating, Janice got up and went to work on Tameka. She lowered her head below her waist and parted her legs. Kissing her lightly at first, as soon as moans started to come from Tameka, Janice parted her other set of lips and lapped at her clitoris with her tongue. Opening her legs even wider, Tameka pushed Janice's head deeper. She loved the way Tameka tasted; it never failed that she herself would orgasm whenever she pleased Tameka. Janice continued to lick and suck on Tameka's clitoris as she inserted two fingers inside of her. This drove Tameka crazy. Feverishly, she pumped her hips into Janice's face as she orgasm over and over again. Tameka collapsed back onto the bed but Janice went around to the other side of the bed and opened the nightstand. Then she pulled out the strap-on dildo. Janice loved when Tameka fucked her with it. Tameka was exhausted and ready to go home to her husband and child. Yet, she never told Janice no. Therefore, she rolled over, got off the bed, and took the strap-on dildo from Janice's hand.

Tameka bent Janice over on the bed, placed one of her legs up on the side of her, then mounted her from behind. Janice hissed in pleasure while she threw her hips toward Tameka's thrusts. Powerfully, Tameka pumped in and out of Janice and playfully smacked her on her butt. This used to be okay with Tameka but that was before she got married. She was madly in love with her husband of less than one year.

Detective Jonathan Harper, also known as Puncho, meant the world to her. If he ever found out what she was doing with her mentor, Judge Janice Matheson, she was certain Puncho would leave her. It wouldn't be because she was having an affair; it would be because she kept a secret from him. Tameka's mind was on her husband as Janice finally orgasm. She thought to herself that she would have to talk to Janice soon about discontinuing their affair. Even though Janice was close to fifty years old, her sexual appetite appeared to be insatiable. She stood from the bed, kissed Tameka on the lips, and walked back into the living-dining room area. Tameka went into the bathroom and started the shower. She got in under the almost scalding hot water and tried to wash away what had taken place. In the beginning, she hadn't felt like this. She scrubbed her skin, in between her legs, then adjusted the water to a cooler temperature as she rinsed off.

With her robe on, Janice was in the kitchen, removing dinner from the oven that she'd purchased for them from Chops. She had started to put it on plates when Tameka came in fully dressed with her purse and keys in her hands. "Baby, wait a minute. Where are you going? I had a romantic dinner planned for us." She took one of the finished plates and placed it on the table.

"I have an assignment to finish; I have class tomorrow night. I'm not going to be able to do any of it at work. The boss has court; therefore, I know I'll be running around like a chicken with my head cut off. Plus, Jonathan got off early today. So, I'd like to spend a little time with him and Londyn."

As soon as Tameka said her husband's name, Janice's face turned sour. "Well, you can just take the food; it should be enough for the three of you. I went out of my way and fought traffic to go to your favorite restaurant so that tonight would be perfect. But it's okay; I have a present for you also." Janice turned around, went to her purse in the living room, and removed a small blue bag. Tameka would recognize that color blue anywhere. It was something from Tiffany & Co. Suddenly, she felt bad because she knew Janice didn't have anyone anymore. Her husband had died three years ago from colon cancer. Janice picked-up the dishes and started to put the food back in the to-go containers. Tameka removed the velvet box from the small, blue gift bag, leaned against the wall, and opened the box. Her breath was taken away. Inside, was a pair of diamond solitaire earrings that had to be at least three or four carats apiece. She looked up at Janice who had just finished packing the food away. "What are these for?"

Janice moved closer to Tameka and reached out to touch her face. "They're just for you being you. You don't like them? We can go this weekend, when you have time, and find something else if these aren't nice enough for you. I thought they would look perfect. Especially, since you've chopped off all of your beautiful hair. They sparkle like your eyes."

Tameka came from the slums of Perry Homes housing projects; her white mother was a heroin junkie who didn't care which neighbor fed her or where she spent the night. She knew what it felt like not to have anything. For that reason, she was appreciative of everything she got. One of the earrings had a stone that was bigger than the one in her wedding ring. She accepted the gift, but wondered what Jonathan would say when he saw them. She might just keep it a secret until her birthday or Christmas. Her phone rang. It was her husband. "Hey baby, I'm on my way home. I have to finish my assignment for school. Then, I'm all yours. I stopped and got us something from Chops. Okay, I'll be safe. See

34

you in a little while." Tameka ended the call. When she looked up, Janice had tears streaming down her face.

"Just go home to your family. Don't worry about me. I think I'll stay here tonight in order to be close to my office. I have court at eight a.m. I love you Tameka." Janice turned, walked out of the kitchen, went into the bedroom, and closed the door.

Tameka dropped the gift bag into her Michael Kors purse, grabbed the food, walked out the door, and then locked it behind her. She felt so bad leaving Janice there alone. Getting into the Lexus that Janice had bought her as a graduation gift, she drove through the parking garage. Tameka knew Janice did a lot for her. To tell the truth, Janice had done more for her since they'd met than her parents, both of whom were drug addicts. She picked up her blackberry and dialed Janice's number. "I'm so sorry that I had to leave you like that; I'll make it up to you."

"You don't have to make anything up to me. It became apparent that you didn't love me as much as I loved you when you got married last year. I'll be okay. Go home to your husband. I'll talk to you later." Janice's feelings were hurt.

"Judge, you're the only woman I've ever been with. Don't act like that. I am not a lesbian; I'm with you because I love you. I don't look at or think about other women. There's only you. I have a son who I've been raising by myself since I was fourteen years old; I want normalcy. This man loved my son before he even met me.

Do you know how difficult that is to find? I was raising a young, black male alone in the inner city. He was a positive influence and took him under his wing long before I even came along. I love Jonathan, which is why I married him–not to try to use him to hide my sexuality. I'm not gay." Tameka had began to raise her voice because she needed Janice to understand that this isn't something she does. She drove out of the garage. As soon as she exited, a police car that was chasing another vehicle, but didn't have its siren or lights on, hit her car.

Chapter 5: Come a Long Way Baby...

Mercedes sat on the exam table dumbfounded. She and her husband, Brandon also known as Money to all of his friends, had been trying to conceive for the past year. She thought they had finally done it. She didn't want to get Money's hopes up, but she was experiencing symptoms such as: lost of appetite, irritability, one of her breasts were sore, and fatigue. Automatically, she assumed she was pregnant at last. This would be a good thing because she'd informed him that if they hadn't conceived by their first anniversary they would go to a fertility doctor. He agreed, but he didn't usually agree with anything that made Mercedes happy.

She wished he was beside her now. However, he was downtown doing the final walk-through in his new club. After all the years of hustling dope and promoting clubs, his dream had finally come true; he had his own and she couldn't have been more proud. Mercedes was supposed to be with him this morning but she woke up feeling bad. She assumed it had a lot to do with her being at Jeezy's video shoot so late last night. Mercedes had come a long way from being the cute chubby girl who could dress. She was now Atlanta's go-to-girl in the fashion world. All of the celebrities and wanna be celebrities wanted to be styled by Mercedes.

The nurse walked back into the room, told her she could put her clothes on, and the doctor would like to talk to her in her office. As soon as the nurse closed the door, Mercedes burst into tears. She couldn't believe this was happening to her. She was finally happy. Her teenage daughter, Heavyn was doing excellent in school. Their relationship couldn't be better. Her job was outstanding; she was getting paid top dollar to do something she loved, she was in love with her best friend, and he was in love with her. Now this shit. A fucking lump in her breast was about to change her life. This is the shit that honestly makes you wonder if there is a God. Mercedes slipped back into her House of Harlow long sleeved maxi dress and put her Fendi wedge heeled booties back on. She went over to the sink in the exam room, splashed her face with cold water, and dried it off with a paper towel. Then, she ran her hands through her bone straight, jet black, shoulder length bob. Finally, she reached into her Fendi Spy bag to remove her oversized shades to hide her eyes.

Peeping in again, the nurse asked was she ready. Mercedes nodded her head up and down. Afraid she might choke on her words, she didn't want to say anything. Mercedes followed her down a short hallway and past the exam rooms. They entered the plush suite which held all of the doctors' offices. The nurse knocked on Dr. Jones' door and was told to come in. Once she entered, the nurse closed the door behind her. "Please have a seat Mercedes. I know you're nervous right now. You came in the office this morning for one reason but we're talking about something totally different. Calm down, everything is going to be alright."

"How can you say everything is going to be alright, Deja? I thought I was pregnant but I could have cancer. Get the fuck out of here. Everything is not all damn right!" Mercedes was so upset. She didn't mean to take her anger out on her friend that she'd grown up with. Knowing even if it wasn't cancer, she still had a massive lump in breast that needed to be removed. Snatching off her shades, she used the back of her hands to wipe her eyes as tears flowed continuously down her face.

Déjà stood up from behind her desk, sat beside her friend, and hugged her tightly. "It's going to be alright, I promise. With one phone call, I'll get you in to see the best oncologist in the south. This is not cancer. It's just a tumor. I want you to go to the lab across the street; I'm about to call them right now. They'll do an emergency biopsy. I'll have my colleague read it. Once again, I'm telling you, you'll be fine." In order to convince herself as well, Déjà repeatedly told Mercedes she would be fine. They had been close friends since they were in fourth grade at C.M. Pitts Elementary School.

"Okay. Do you think I should call Money and tell him what's going on, or should I wait? The most fucked up part about all of this is cancer could have run in either my mother's or father's side of the family—or both. But I don't know shit about them because I was left on the steps of a fucking church!" Mercedes kicked the desk in front of her so hard that she left a footprint in the wood. "I'll get that fixed."

"The procedure won't take that long. Since I don't have another patient until after eleven, I can go over there with you. You and Money can talk about it when he gets home later. Everything is going to be alright." Déjà rubbed Mercedes' back then went back around to her desk to call the lab. She informed them she was bringing a patient over right away for a breast biopsy.

As soon as her friend hung up the phone, Mercedes laughed and asked, "do you keep saying everything is going to be alright so that you can convince yourself? 'Cause bitch it's not working for me."

"Girl whatever. Let's go across this street. Have you found me something to wear to the grand opening of Luxurious yet? You know I have to be a "Baddie" up in that piece. Plus, I'm trying to find me a husband honey." Déjà removed her white lab coat then put on a black leather L.A.M.B. motorcycle jacket which made her outfit look entirely different. Taking off her glasses, she placed them in the case and put it inside her purse. She didn't even need the glasses. However, she felt they made her look older and more professional.

"I have some looks on my iPad that I'll show you later. Every one is asking me to style them for this event, which is good. Most people don't even know that Money is my husband so I'm busy all the way around the board with this event. He is definitely bringing the city out, not to mention he has the "who's who" of entertainment and sports flying in. It's definitely going to be a night to remember." Mercedes was just as excited as her husband about the grand opening of his club.

They stopped at the front desk before leaving the office building so that Déjà could tell the administrative assistant she was taking Mercedes over herself. They caught the elevator downstairs. Even though the light was red, the two women ran across Peachtree Street and rushed into the front doors of Emory Crawford Long Hospital. As they caught the elevator up to the lab, Mercedes' phone rang, she looked down, and saw that it was Money calling. Pressing the ignore button, she exited the elevator after Déjà and followed her down the hallway. They went right into the laboratory. The doctor pointed to the room that he wanted Mercedes to go into. "Please go in, remove your clothes, and put on the hospital gown that is lying on the table. I will be right in." Mercedes went in; the doctor turned to Déjà and said "Jones, this must be a bad case if you bought her over immediately."

"Lee, I prescribed her some hormones earlier in the year, after her annual. She was trying to get pregnant. Everything was fine; she had a perfect pap, labs, and mammogram. Today, she comes in feeling sluggish, loss of appetite, and her breasts are sore. We both thought she was pregnant. But she has a huge lump in her breast that just doesn't feel right. She's been my friend since

41

elementary; she's very special to me. I couldn't let her go through this alone." Déjà told the older Japanese doctor.

They walked into the small room. Mercedes was sitting on the table with the hospital gown on. "Okay, well let's get this show on the road. I'm going to use a local anesthetic to numb the area. Then, I will go in with this needle. Don't be afraid, you will only feel a pinch. The cultures will be sent next door. Jones will have the results in twenty-four to forty-eight hours." The doctor stated with barely any accent.

Déjà walked around to the other side of the table, took Mercedes' hand, and held it tightly. They both watched as Dr. Lee stuck the long needle into Mercedes' right breast and removed some fluid. As the needle filled with a bloody fluid, tears rolled down Déjà's face. It was the first sign that something was definitely wrong.

Chapter 6: BawSe Man

Whyte rode around the city with so much on his mind. Ever since he had come back from New York, he had been moving more than three times the amount of weight than usual. Normally, that would be a good thing. However, he had to bring in more workers, which meant more people that he had to watch over. Chrissy had a minor complication with her surgery. Therefore, he had to look after her. At present, she was back at one hundred percent. It seemed like he had too much on his plate. Nonetheless, he was use to challenges.

He had learned long ago, in the dope game, everyone is not gonna like you. On the other hand, everyone is not gon' hate you either. Whyte had managed to stay under the radar. Yet, in the last six months, it seemed like even when people didn't know he was the actual man, he was still hearing his name. That was definitely not a good thing. He never affiliated himself with this new shit in Atlanta—with the gangs and cliques. He tried to keep that shit out of his organization; he had since come to find out that some of his top earners were now bangin' or hangin' with the bangers. Therefore, Whyte called a meeting at the new club Luxurious which

Money was preparing to open. Whyte was a silent partner in it.

The parking lot was full like the club was already operational. He recognized many of the cars as staff and some of his associates. Whyte parked his all white Range Rover in the handicap spot in the front, jumped out and went inside the club. He walked through the upper level then went downstairs to the boom-boom room. Everybody was sitting around smoking Kush. Some were playing pool and others watching sports highlights on ESPN. There was a nude girl in the corner dancing on the pole. A few of the guys were throwing money at her as she danced to Birdman's Rich Gang new hit single, "Tapout." He cleared his throat as he took his cell phone out and called Money to come downstairs. When he ended his call, everyone acknowledged him properly. Whyte silently thought to himself, "now-a-days, it felt like he was babysitting a whole bunch of grown folks."

Money walked into the room with a glass of clear liquid in his hand. Everyone except Dent, who had his attention focused on the girl that was working the pole, greeted him. Or at least, that's what he wanted Money to think. In actuality, he couldn't stand Dent. He only put up with him because of how close he and Whyte were. Money cleared his throat and said loudly to the dancer. "You should be over on the other side of the room dancing for his girl; she's the one with all the money and hustle. He just looks like he's the one who's got it."

Everyone in the room looked over at Jordyn who was sitting on the stool, off to herself, smoking a blunt, and drinking a mini bottle of Sutter Homes Moscato. "Don't send her over here Money. Shit, I already got one bitch that won't stay out of my damn pockets." Jordyn's eyes shot daggers in her baby daddy's direction.

As Whyte called the meeting to order, the tension in the air was thick. "Okay y'all, cool out. This is the first time I've been able to bring the old and new team together. I'm sure all y'all already know each other; so let's get down to business. It's some shit going on in these streets and I don't like it. I'm just trynna stay focused on getting money. I lay in the cut, don't wear flashy jewelry, and don't fuck a lot of hoes. I don't be out in the clubs or on the scene. I'm forty-one years old and I've never been locked up–not even for a traffic violation. I don't like all this unnecessary attention y'all drawin' to this crew. I move in silence. Now I understand you like nice things, you've made money, and now you wanna spend it. I understand you have friends outside of the crew that you wanna be around. That's all well and good, but don't let all your flexing and pillow talking be my downfall."

"It's them young niggas that's doin' everything, big homie. They're so happy to be on a winning team, they stay screaming your name. Then, they gang bangin', or whatever you wanna call it, 'cause Atlanta don't have any real damn gang bangers." Dent interrupted him with his outburst.

"Nigga, sit your five dolla ass down before I make change. You stay screaming Whyte's name more than you say your own. Shit, you need to be screaming my name like that. You hang out with Whyte, but nigga you live, eat, and shit because of me. You're the only one in here that ain't working. Why in the fuck are you here anyway? This meeting ain't for cheerleaders. It's a team meeting between the coach and players." Jordyn stayed chumping off Dent, and there was nothing he could do but take it. He used to beat on her. After she shot him in his foot, the last thing on his mind was putting his hands on her.

"Well damn, looks like she's spoken." Pick said as he walked over and took the blunt out of Jordyn's hand.

"Don't be ribbing her ass up. Nigga you supposed to be my mother fucking brother." Dent said to his younger brother, who also worked for Whyte.

"He ain't ribbing me up. Everybody in here knows you're nothin' but a cheerleader, which is all fine and good. The bad thing is nigga you shaking those pom-poms for the wrong mother fucker on the team." Jordyn hated that Dent never acknowledged all she did for him. Then again, the people in this room knew he was actually the man behind the woman instead of it being vice versa.

"See, this is the shit I'm talking about. We're too busy focusing on the wrong thing. I didn't call this meeting for you two to be arguing over who's the boss. We need to be focused on the organization and the logistics for the grand opening of the club. Jordyn, you shouldn't even care what other people think. As long as the people that matter know you're running everything, that's all that counts!" Whyte did something that he never did. He raised his voice as he ran his hands through his blonde curls.

"Dat's right homie! Shit, everybody know Jordyn run the show." Money was taking pleasure in seeing Dent made fun of in front of everyone. He despised the way Dent was living off of Jordyn's money and the fame of the team.

Dent sat and stared intensely at Jordyn. He leaped out of his chair and tackled Money. They fell back onto the pool table. "Fat motherfucker, you always gotta run your mouth. Let's see how fast it runs after I bust your lip.

Instead of breaking it up, Whyte stepped out of the way. Julio jumped up from the sofa to try to help Money. But Whyte held out his arm to block Julio—allowing them to fight it out. "Let they ass fight. These two niggas argue like bitches every time they're in the same room with each other. They might as well get this shit off their chest. It was bound to happen."

"I came here to talk about business and what's going on in the organization. Not to see the circus act. I already get enough of being around this clown." Jordyn grabbed her Berkin bag, got up, and walked out of the room. She left the club and went to her truck. As she was getting in, Goldie was approaching.

"Hey Jay, where you going? Don't tell me the meeting's over already." Goldie had been in Etheridge Court fighting with his baby momma, Raquel all evening. It took him forever to convince her to let him leave the house.

"Man, I don't know what them folks got going on in there. It didn't look like they were discussing any business to me. I don't have time for all that fuckin' shit. I have enough on my plate already. I'm about to go to Spondivits, sit down, have me a bite to eat, a few shots, and enjoy my own damn company." Jordyn got in her truck and closed the door.

"Shit, if they ain't talking about nothin', I'm going with you." Goldie walked around and got in on the passenger's side of Jordyn's truck. He had liked her since he first started working for Whyte, but didn't let on because of Dent. Jordyn was a good girl; she deserved so much more than Dent's trifling ass. And Goldie was about to show her.

Dent was exiting the side door of the club when he saw Goldie hop in the truck with Jordyn and pull off. He called her phone as he walked rapidly to his car. A recording came on telling him the number he had reached was out of service.

He mumbled to himself between clinched teeth, "that bitch better not be taking that nigga to my motherfucking house. I see I'mma have to start back beating her ass again." Mad at the world, Dent got into his car and headed in the direction of the house. Just as he was about to get on the expressway at Tenth Street, the police jumped behind him and pulled him over.

Chapter 7: Pretty is as Pretty Does...

In her BMW X6, Chrissy sat in front of Essential Essence, her spa and full service salon. She was praying and meditating before she walked through the doors. Every morning, she made it her business to perform that ritual before she went in. Because she dealt with so many different people and assorted attitudes, she found it helped her to get through her day. Her cell phone vibrated. She looked down and saw it was Whyte. After all these years, just the thought of him gave her butterflies. "Hey bae. What's up?"

"I'm just trying to figure out why my wife left the house and didn't wake me up. Haven't I told your ass about doing that? Anything can happen during the course of a day. If I'm home, I'm supposed to see your face each and every day." Because he picked up the phone and called her as soon as he noticed she wasn't there, Whyte's voice was groggy.

"Daviyd, I'm sorry," which was his birth name. Chrissy apologized. Besides his parents, she was the only one that called him that.

"I'll make it up to you; I promise bae. Maybe, I'll leave the shop early; I'll call you later on. Love you with all of me." Chrissy had to meet with the real estate agent about some condos that she was purchasing as investment properties. Her plan was to leave her meeting and take Whyte out to lunch. Ever since she'd recovered from her plastic surgery, he was on her like butter on hot rice. He had to know her every move and who she was with. She didn't mind; it let her know he wanted her.

"Love you baby, until the death of me." He hung up the phone, rolled over in their California king sized platform bed, and pulled the covers over his head. He wished he could take a break for just a day. Unfortunately, he couldn't because even though he had everyone together last night, nothing had been accomplished. In fact, the shit had gotten worst. He had gotten a call about some more shit.

Chrissy sat in her truck and said a silent prayer for both of them to have a prosperous, safe day. It seemed she couldn't get him out of the streets. No matter how hard she tried. He had been telling her he was going to retire this year. However, she didn't see that in his near future. He was moving more dope now than he ever had. They didn't have children and she refused to as long as her husband was still in the streets. When he wasn't in the bed beside her, she could barely sleep at night. The streets of Atlanta were getting worse and worse. Most of all his homeboys that he hung out with, when she first met him all those years ago, were either dead or in jail. The last thing Chrissy wanted to do was bury her husband. She would have to die with him because without him, there is no her.

A silver BMW 650 convertible pulled up in the parking spot beside her. Doing breathing exercises, Chrissy continued to sit behind the tinted windows in the peace and quiet. Somehow, she had a feeling this was going to be a chaotic day. She watched as her best friend, Pretty got out of the car with three boxes from the Krispy Kreme doughnut shop. He walked up to her car window and started hollering in his high-pitched voice. "Bitch, I see your black ass behind all of that tint. I left the door open, get the coffee off the backseat and come on in here honey so I can pour you the tea Miss Thang."

Chrissy closed her eyes and took one last deep breath before getting out of the truck. Something just didn't feel right about today. She woke up feeling that way; she tried to shake it off. She hoped her day got better.

Pretty was emptying the boxes and putting the doughnuts and pastries on a serving tray. Chrissy honestly couldn't imagine her life without him. She referred to him as her gay husband. They had met during their freshmen year at Kennesaw State University. He wasn't called Pretty then; he was going by his birth name, Dylan. They took three classes together but had never spoken up until the day she came to school with her hair freshly done.

He stated, "girl you need to quit letting them people put all that *Pump It Up* spritz in your hair. That is so nineties. You need a soft look. You have a pretty round face and a lot of hair. I could do you a nice roller wrap; it would fall perfectly around your face."

"You do hair?" She had never heard him speak. His voice was very high for him to be a man.

"Girl yes, I do everybody's hair on the Westside. Where you from? You need to come over my house this week. I can hook you up. If you keep letting whoever's doing your hair, put all that spritz in it, it's gon' start to break off."

"I'm from the Westside, but I moved away last year. Can you do it today? I only have two classes and then I'm free all day." Chrissy had always thought to herself that she hated those hard hair do's. She wanted her hair to have bounce and body. Since she had been in the ninth grade, she'd been going to the same girl. All she did was hard hairstyles and weaves.

The two of them left school later on that day and have been inseparable ever since. Pretty was only attending college to make his mother happy, but his heart was in doing hair and makeup. He hadn't come out the closet yet. He simply did all he could to keep his mother happy. She had sacrificed so much to make sure he had everything he wanted.

Chrissy urged him to come out of the closet after she met his mother and fell in love with her. She told him his mother would love and accept him no matter what.

Chrissy was right. When Pretty came out, his mother said she had been waiting on him to be honest with himself. Since he was a little boy, she'd known he was different. The next semester, he dropped out of college and enrolled in Paul Mitchell's hair school and began dressing more flamboyantly.

"Bitch, what is wrong with you? You act like your best friend has died or something and ain't nothing wrong with me. Why are you in slow motion today? Eat a doughnut and drink that cappuccino. Let me tell you about what has been going on. Girl, wait until you hear this."

Chrissy sat in her chair as Pretty moved around the shop in his tight Rock & Republic jeans and fitted button down shirt. He bought all his clothes in the women's section, but never wore dresses or skirts. His clothes fit his slim frame perfectly. He was shaped like a runway model—long and lean. Yet, his face was the showstopper. His flawless, chocolate skin, full lips, big slanted eyes, and naturally curly, jet-black hair is why everyone called him Pretty. As he walked to his workstation, he handed her a cheese Danish, then began to unpack his bag.

"Okay, so you know Jeezy's video shoot was the other night, right? I was the hairstylist hired for the shoot. Girl, oh my god, let me tell you these Atlanta niggas are so fake. They in the street hustling like they're all hard and shit but they're taking more dick than I am." Pretty smacked his lips as he looked over at Chrissy sipping on her cappuccino.

"Honey, this is Atlanta. I'm used to that. Tell me something I don't know." Chrissy had finished her Danish. Now she had a funny taste in her mouth and was attempting to get it out by sipping on the mocha-flavored cappuccino.

"Well, if you give me a chance, I will tell you. Damn! Okay, last night at the shoot you know there were a lot of industry folk there. At least, people who want to make you think they're in the business. Dude's ass was there with all the lil' niggas on his record label. They were putting on real bad. Honey chile, he was driving a Ferrari and everything. So, there was a scene in the video where they're in the V.I.P. at Gigi's Pleasure Chest and throwing money while the strippers is dancing. Girl, this nigga just got to be extra. He started throwing his own money. The production assistant had handed out fake money for everybody to throw. He told them no. Girl, I could have died."

"Dude has always been extra. I think he be overcompensating 'cause he's short or something. I don't know. Maybe he was getting excited because of the girls stripping. You know his wife used to be a stripper. He met her at the club." Chrissy said as her mouth filled with vomit. Jumping up, she ran to her office in the back where she had a private restroom.

Pretty watched Chrissy run through the shop, threw his Danish in the trash, and said out loud, "if that shit is making her sick, I ain't touching it."

Chrissy made it to the restroom just in time. All the contents of her stomach were coming up and she had broken out into a sweat. Before she went to wash her mouth out and brush her teeth, she stood over the toilet and waited to see if anymore was going to come up. She spit in the toilet, flushed it, and then looked in the mirror. She didn't look good. Perhaps, that's why she was moving in slow motion; she could be coming down with something.

Chrissy washed her face and brushed her teeth, applied a light coat of gloss to her lips, and walked back into the salon. After looking down at her Rolex, she saw it was eight a.m. The rest of her team should be here by now. Pretty had his first customer and was putting a cape around her.

"Bitch, are you okay? After I saw that, I threw mine away. I don't need any damn food poisoning. Well anyway, chile sit back down so I can finish telling you."

Chrissy went to the mini fridge and got a small bottle of ginger ale. She came back and sat down to hear what Pretty had to say. "Okay, go ahead and finish honey 'cause I see you not gon' let me have any peace until you tell your piece."

Pretty smacked his lips like he always did. "Let me see, where did I leave off at… Oh yeah, so anyway Dude is throwing his real money and shit when Jeezy is not even throwing real money. It seemed like he was trying to overshadow this man at his own video shoot. So Jeezy pulled him to the side, had a word with him, and they straightened that out. But during one of the breaks, I hear Dude getting fly at the mouth–talking to his lil' flunkies he calls artists. He was dogging Jeezy out. When they started back taping, girl, I heard one of the niggas that be with Jeezy say something like *'don't nobody care about Dude's pussy ass anyway and I mean that literally.'*

"Was my husband there during all of this? Because he and Jeezy are real cool, and you know Dude is his partner." Chrissy wanted to make sure Whyte wasn't caught up in none of this bullshit. Her Blackberry rang and she pulled it out of her pocket without looking at the caller I.D. "Good morning, this is Chrissy."

"Good morning Chrissy, I don't know if I should call you my wife-in-law or step-mommy. I just hope you're good with kids." The female on the other line said before hanging up.

Chrissy stared at her phone then pulled it away from her face. She went into her incoming calls to see who it was. The number said Ontario, Canada. She pushed the send button. A recording came on saying it was a Google voice number, to leave a message, and it will be delivered to the party that you are trying to reach. Chrissy spoke forcefully into the phone. "Bitch, I will tell you what you can call me. Call me Chrissy, 'cause fucking with me they gon' be calling you dead. Two things I don't play about is my husband and my money. You should have checked my resume before you chose to play with me. I always win and don't know what playing fair means."

Pretty looked up at Chrissy who had a sour look on her face. He already knew it was one of Whyte's bitches. Over the years, there had been many. Consequently, that's what came with niggas with money–a lot of women. Obviously, they had gotten ahold of her cell phone number again. "Can I continue? Girl, you know if Whyte was there I would have called you as soon as I saw him, just on general principle. Anyway, let me finish telling you. Damn, you keep interrupting me. So, when the boy said that about Dude, one of his lil' groupies pulls out a red flag and start doing all kind of gang signs. Girl, I could have fainted 'cause you know Jeezy and 'em wear them blue flags. I was praying for my life then. Dude calmed his flunky down and they left. After they left, I heard this queen who was on the shoot that I know from the clubs say to her friend, *"let me call my baby, Dude to make sure he's okay, 'cause he got a temper out of this world."*

Chrissy sat in the chair in total shock. She was already pissed because bitches were calling her early in the morning. But now this shit. Dude was one of Whyte's closest friends. Actually, he was one of the ones from the beginning that was still around. Dude was married to a beautiful woman, and making moves with his studio and record label. She shook her head. Damn, Pretty always had all the news. She thought to herself... It could be worse. At least, Whyte was cheating with females.

"Don't sit there like you're in shock. You just said yourself this is Atlanta. It makes sense now. Last Sunday, when I was at club Miami, I saw a different queen getting into the same Ferrari that Dude was in the other night at the video shoot."

"Okay, okay, okay! Don't tell me anymore. I'm already throwing up as is." Chrissy looked at Pretty in pure disbelief as he worked on his client. She knew he wasn't lying because that was one thing he didn't do.

"Have you had anyone to pull some pieces for the grand opening yet?" Pretty said to Chrissy as he directed his customer to the shampoo bowl area in the back of the salon.

"I have some things that I've had my eye on. But you know I'm so fresh, I don't need a stylist." As she headed to the facial area, Chrissy popped her collar and licked her tongue out at Pretty. Her first customer of the day had walked in.

Chapter 8: Before it's Too Late...

Mercedes woke up on the sofa with sunlight streaming through the window. The marble coffee table was filled with magazines, fabric samples, her iPad, a notepad, and her MacBook Pro. When she got home from lunch with Deja, she began to work on some looks for the grand opening. She took the pill that Déjà gave her after her head wouldn't stop hurting. She didn't even remember lying down on the sofa. Waiting on Money to come home, she must have dozed off. Mercedes got up and stretched. She must have slept hard because she didn't even see or hear her husband when he came in. As she walked down the hallway of the condo, she heard Money arguing over the phone with someone.

"Man, I don't give a fuck what you say. That nigga Dent ain't shit. I don't even know why in the fuck Whyte keep his dick-riding ass around anyway. He fucked up last night when he put his motherfucking hands on me. The pussy nigga act like I was telling a lie; he is a bitch. He's Whyte's bitch and Jordyn pays his salary. I hear what you're sayin' but I gotta do something to him. There were too many of us in that room that know what went down. I can't let that shit go. Then it will seem like I'm some type of bitch ass nigga. We know that's not the case." Money was on the phone with his right-hand man, Julio.

Mercedes had heard enough. She opened the door all the way and went inside. Her husband was sitting up in the bed with his back against the headboard of the ceiling high, quilted, white leather headboard that she had designed. He didn't have on a shirt and his entire upper body was filled with tattoos. His nearly jet-black skin contrasted with the stark white of the headboard. After all these years, she was still in love with this man. She took her dress off, pulled the covers back, and got into bed with him. He pulled her close and started to run his hands up and down her back as he continued the phone call. Mercedes laid her head on his chest and took a deep breath. She wanted to be optimistic. However, she knew she had cancer. Although the results hadn't come back yet, she knew. While the doctor was doing the biopsy, she had seen the tears as they flowed from Déjà's eyes. She pretended she didn't.

Money ended the call with Julio, reached down, and started rubbing his wife's hair. "You were tired last night. I tried to wake you up, but you wouldn't budge. I had to check your pulse."

"Why didn't you pick me up and bring me in here with you then?" Mercedes raised her head and looked him in his eyes.

"I don't know; I should have. You were sleeping so peacefully though. I figured you were tired; I know you didn't get home from the video shoot until the wee hours of the morning."

"Yes, I guess I was more tired than I realized. I actually sat on the couch after helping Heavyn with her homework then worked a little bit. I was really waiting on you to come in." Mercedes rubbed his muscular chest and put her leg on top of his.

"Well, it looks like sleep took over because when I came in, you were dead to the world. You didn't even hear her when she left out this morning to catch the school bus. It was like you had taken a sleeping pill or something." Money's phone started to ring. He picked it up and looked at it. It was Whyte. Usually, he would answer, but not this time. He hadn't had time to spend with Mercedes in two days. Putting the phone back down, he started to rub on her leg and butt.

Mercedes began speaking. "Baby, we have to talk. There's something I need to tell you. I had been feeling run down so I went to see Déjà yesterday."

Money's phone rang again; it was Whyte again. "Baby hold that thought, this must be an emergency if this nigga keep calling." He picked up the phone. Whyte was frantic on the other line. "Okay my nigga. I'm on my way." Money pushed Mercedes' leg off of him and jumped from the bed. He still had the phone to his ear. "Yeah, I'm putting my clothes on right now. Meet me at the barbershop." Money dressed frantically as Mercedes watched him. She would just have to tell him later. Rolling over in the bed, she pulled the covers up over her head.

Money went into the bathroom. Mercedes heard the water run, him brushing his teeth, and then he came out. She remained hidden under the covers. He pulled them back, bent down, and kissed her gently. "Ewwww, morning breath. I'll be back in a little while; we can talk then. You don't have to work today do you?"

"No, I don't. I'm thinking about going to the spa though. I need to take a load off. Either call me or I'll see you when I get back." Mercedes felt the tears about to come so she pulled the covers back over her head.

"Tonight, we can go out somewhere for dinner. You can get dressed up. Have you already figured out what we're wearing to the grand opening next week?" He pulled out a wad of money, peeled off half of it, and left it on the nightstand for his wife. Money walked out of their bedroom.

Mercedes said a silent prayer every time her husband walked out of the door. He had finally gotten the club that he always wanted and was supposed to be out of the streets for good. Yet, she knew he wasn't. Whenever Whyte called, Money went running. She knew Whyte had put up half of the money for the club. Therefore, maybe her husband felt he owed him something. Perhaps, after the grand opening next week, she would see a difference. Each time she said something to him about it, his reply was always *"I'm always gonna be a street nigga."* Her cell phone was ringing but she had left it in her purse which was in the living room. Whoever it was, she would call back later. She simply wanted to sleep and get everything off her mind.

Chapter 9: One Man, Two Lives

Jonathan received the call that his wife had been in a car accident with a patrol car. He rushed to Grady Memorial Hospital. He jumped out of his department issued Ford Taurus in the parking space for emergency vehicles. Tameka had been on her way home to him when she had the accident. He hoped it wasn't serious and she wasn't hurt.

Tameka was conscious but had a major headache. She didn't remember anything except being on the phone with the judge. As she was pulling out of the parking garage, she had looked both ways. Nonetheless, she was hit. She had blacked out. Now she was strapped down on a gurney in the hallway of the emergency room with a neck brace on her neck, and her head bandaged. Her mouth was dry. It seemed as if the more time passed, the more pain she felt. A nurse passing by stopped as Tameka moaned. "Hey baby, are you okay?"

"No, I'm in a lot of pain. I'm very cold and extremely thirsty." Tameka barely spoke above a whisper.

"Okay, well it's a little bit warmer in the rooms. You're in the hall because they're about to take you to have an MRI done to make sure everything is alright. I just ordered you an I.V. bag. Don't worry, everything will be okay." The nurse walked away and returned with two warm blankets which she placed over Tameka.

"Thank you." She whispered through her chapped lips. Her face hurt. All she wanted was her husband; she needed him urgently. She hoped the nurse would come back and check on her soon. Then she could ask her to please call her husband.

Jonathan didn't stop at the admissions desk. He flashed his badge and walked straight through to the emergency room. He didn't know what had happened; he was waiting on his wife to get home. The next thing he knew, someone had called to say they heard over the radio that his wife had been in a car accident downtown. His heart beat wildly as he walked frantically down the long hospital corridors to the emergency room. Once he finally arrived, once again, he flashed his badge to the security guard, then opened the double doors to the emergency room. It was extremely chaotic and loud as nurses and doctors rushed about. Approaching the nurse's station, he provided his wife's name.

Tameka knew her husband's rich, baritone voice anywhere. She attempted to call out his name but all that came out was a whisper. She was strapped down to the gurney in a manner that wouldn't allow her to turn her head in his direction. She just laid there waiting for the nurse to hopefully point him in her direction, which seemed to be only four or five feet away.

Jonathan stared at the nurse while she put his wife's name in the computer. He remembered the first day he had met her. He was working with the younger group of boys at Adamsville Recreation Center; he volunteered there in his spare time. It was the same neighborhood he had grown up in without a father. Typically, he worked with the teenagers. They had gone on a field trip on this particular day. Therefore, he was in the computer lab assisting the younger boys with their homework.

Jonathan was crouched over the desk assisting a nine year old who was getting more and more frustrated by the minute with his homework. "I don't see why I need to learn this math stuff anyway. I know how to count money and that's all that matters. I'mma be a rapper. So all I really need to know is how to sell drugs and get a lot of girls." The young man said it with a determined look in his eyes. That frightened Jonathan. Twenty years ago, he was that same little boy–with a single mother and no father. He had to do something to stop this. Jonathan knew he wasn't the best person in the world, but he certainly hoped he did enough good to balance it out.

He took the boy named, Londyn under his wing and spent time with him. It wasn't long before he met his mother during an awards ceremony which was sponsored by the police department for the after-school program. Tameka had just come from her internship at the law firm. She wasn't what Jonathan expected at all. He fell in love at first sight.

He snapped out of his reverie as the nurse informed him his wife was on a gurney in front of exam room twelve. "Why is she in front of the exam room instead of inside of it?" He shouted to the nurse who jumped at the force in his voice. "Grady Hospital ain't shit!" Jonathan left the desk to go and look for exam room twelve.

Tameka was trying to keep her eyes open; she was so drowsy. She heard her husband's footsteps approaching. Her heart started to flutter. He had this affect on her. Without a doubt, she knew he was her forever.

"Baby, are you alright? What happened?" The pain that Jonathan saw in his wife's eyes–he wanted to take it away. He reached down, grasped her hand, and rubbed it. Then he bent to kiss her forehead. "Don't worry; everything will be alright. Let me call the judge to let her know what has happened. Where is your doctor? I need to see what's going on."

Part of Tameka wanted to know why the judge hadn't arrived at the hospital yet. There was no possible way she didn't know what was going on. She was on the phone with her when it happened. The collision was so loud, that it seemed all the occupants of the building had come out front to see what was going on. Not to mention, they were on the phone with one another when the car hit her. It didn't matter, as long as her husband was there with her.

Jonathan's phone rang. He looked down at it. "Baby, this is the boss. I need to take this call." With his cell phone to his ear, he walked away from his wife.

"Hey man, I need you. Some big shit has come up. Meet us at the barbershop." Whyte said to his friend.

"Man, I can't! Tameka was just in a car accident. I'm down here at Grady right now." Jonathan hated the fact that when Whyte called, he expected him to jump. This was the one time he was going to have to take care of business without him.

"I need you in on this. It can't wait. You won't be gone no more than thirty minutes. I'll see you when you get here." Whyte hung up the phone.

Jonathan looked over at his wife on the gurney and knew he couldn't leave her alone. In spite of this, he also had to tend to the business with Whyte. He dialed the judge's number and waited for her to answer. He could get her to come and sit with Tameka while he went to the short meeting. "Hey judge, this is Harper. Tameka was in a car accident on her way home. She's conscious and they're running tests on her right now. I just had a big break in a case that I'm working on. I was wondering if you could come and sit with her for an hour while I go and meet with this witness." He listened to the judge, then hung up the phone. The judge was a lifesaver. He went back to his wife.

"Is everything okay?" Tameka whispered when her husband grabbed her hand again. He had a lot of worry in his eyes as he stood over her and rubbed her hair.

"I just got a break in a big case that I've been working on. I have to go and talk to someone, but I won't be gone for long. The judge is on her way here so that you're not alone." Living two lives was getting the best of him. Jonathan didn't want to leave his wife at the hospital, but he had to.

Chapter 10: A Little Taste of Your Own Medicine

Dent sat in the holding cell and used his cell phone. He was still in shock that he had been locked up for stealing his own car. He tried to explain to the officer that it was his car, but in his girl's name. However, the white cop wasn't trying to hear it. Dialing her number yet again, he continued to get the same recording that he got before he pulled out of the parking lot. He called Whyte's phone, it went straight to voicemail as well. Therefore, he hung up.

He stood and began to pace back and forth. His mind was going a hundred miles a minute. All kinds of thoughts ran through his mind. He couldn't believe Jordyn was creeping with Goldie. Dent shook the thought from his head. She could've just been giving him a ride. Yet, his car was in the parking lot too. Goldie was too young for Jordyn. She didn't even like young men. At least, that's what she always told Dent.

The cell started to vibrate in his hand. He looked down and saw that it was Apple. He didn't even feel like talking to her right now. Dent had put it in his mind that he was going to leave this girl alone and try to focus on his family. On the other hand, there was something about the way she fucked him that made him so weak for her. He answered the phone. "Yeah, what's up baby?"

"I've been calling you all day. You said you were gonna take me to the mall and get me those Red Bottoms for T.I.'s album release party tomorrow. Daddy you know I've got to out-shine all them bitches in there. I represent you when I step out. How am I gonna fuck with a boss but walk around looking like the help?" Apple's squeaky, soft voice told Dent exactly what he wanted to hear.

"Look ma, I just got banged up. Something's wrong with the paperwork on my car. I'm trying to get out of here. Don't worry, you're gonna be the flyest bitch in the party. Come on down to Rice Street and get me out."

"You must have the money on you 'cause I just paid my rent and won't have any cash until I go to work tomorrow." Apple wasn't about to spend her funds to get Dent out of jail. She didn't even wanna be the one to go and pick him up. He had gotten too comfortable with her. All this shit he was asking was in his baby momma's job description, not hers.

"Naw, I ain't got no money on me. I had just dropped off the money at my spot and was on my way home." Dent had her thinking he was Whyte's partner.

"Well, I know you don't want me to call your baby momma. Besides, she doesn't have any money anyway. You want me to go and pick up some from Whyte?" Apple really wanted to fuck with Whyte. Unfortunately, he didn't pay her any attention. From what she had seen, he appeared to be faithful to his wife, who was a plain Jane compared to Apple.

"Just stay by your phone, I have some calls to make. I might need you to go somewhere and pick up some money then come and get me." Dent hung up the phone with Apple as fast as he could. This broke bitch couldn't even give him a little money to get out of jail. Her squeaky ass baby voice urked the hell out of him. He tried to call Whyte one more time. This time, he answered on the first ring.

"What's up my nigga? Y'all was wildin' at the club. I just let y'all battle it out since you've been at each other's neck for a minute now. The pressure had to be released eventually." Whyte knew that the fight earlier was just the beginning between Dent and Money. He was going to have a sit down with the two of them to end it, or else they'd fight every time they saw one another.

"Dat bitch reported the car stolen. I got pulled over right before I got on the highway. I'm locked up and something's wrong with her phone. Can you send somebody down here to get me? I can't spend the night in this motherfucker."

"Yeah, I got some folks that own some bonding companies. I'll call them as soon as I get off with you and have them put a card in for you." Whyte thought to himself maybe Jordyn really has gotten tired of Dent leaching off of her.

"'Preciate it my nigga. Whatever it cost, I'll make sure you get it right back, as soon as I hit the streets." Dent was happy that Whyte was sending someone to come and get him. As soon as he got home, he planned on beating Jordyn's ass.

Dent heard some commotion outside as he slipped his phone back in his pocket. He sat down on the steel bench attached to the wall.

"Pussy nigga. You know you don't wanna see me on the streets. My name holds weight in this city. You must not be from around here? You don't know who I am? Young nigga get a badge without a gun and think he can muscle me around. If I make it upstairs, your punk ass will not make it back down!"

The detention officer was not paying the inmate any attention. He wasn't from Atlanta or affiliated with anyone. Therefore, he didn't know he was pushing around the head of the largest set of Bloods in the city. He shoved him inside of the holding cell and pulled the door closed with a bang.

Head sat down on the opposite bench. He looked up at Dent then hung his head low. His baldhead was perspiring and his eyes were bloodshot. "Dat nigga can't be from the A' handlin' me like I'm some regular Joe Blow." He said aloud but was talking to himself.

Dent hoped that whoever Whyte had called was on the way. He pulled out his phone and called Whyte again. This time, it went straight to voicemail. He left a message. "Aye, 'preciate you again bruh. I hope them folks on the way; I ain't trynna go upstairs in this bitch."

Head saw him with the phone. His eyes lit up. "Aye partna, let me make a phone call real quick. I'm trynna get up out this muthafucka my damn self. I couldn't get my phone off the charger before I got pulled over.

Dent heard the cocky man who was sitting in front of him. He looked up at him with one eyebrow raised.

"Allow me to introduce myself. I'm Head. What they call you my nigga?"

Dent looked at Head. He was big with a baldhead. He had a baseball hat cocked on his head with a B on it. From head to toe, he was dressed in all black except for the red bottoms on his shoes. Instantly, he knew who he was. This was Head out of Cali. Right before they closed them down, he had taken over Capitol Homes. Furthermore, he was the leader of the Bloods. He leaned over to hand his iPhone to him. "My name is Dent my nigga, Westside Dent."

"'Preciate it my nigga." He dialed a number and waited for someone to come on the line. "Yo ma', holla at yo people and tell 'em to pull me. I'll be waitin'." He ended the call and handed the phone back to Dent. "You Whyte's people right?"

"Yeah, I'm his right-hand man." Dent said proudly.

"Nah, you might be his underhand man, but Money is the right-hand. I'm just fucking with you. I know who you are my nigga. I wouldn't have made it this far without knowing all the players in the game, and the water boys too." Head recognized that Dent was nothing more than a certified cheerleader. He wasn't making any power moves.

A female correction officer came to the door and escorted Dent to be finger printed. She happened to notice his cell phone bulging from his pocket, took it from him, and stated she'd be placing it with the rest of his property.

The hours ticked away slowly. Dent was pissed beyond belief. For the past four hours, he had paced the holding cell. His anger mounted every time he called someone collect and couldn't get through. He realized Whyte said he would get him out, but it seemed to be taking forever. Maybe his partner had turned his back on him just like Jordyn had. Shit, he didn't even help him when he and Money got to fighting at the club. He merely sat there and watched with his arms folded. With his frustration mounting, he yelled "man fuck all dem niggas," as he hung up the phone, and walked back over to the steel bench.

Head had his back up against the wall, with his feet up, watching Dent and his theatrics. He hadn't said anything else since Dent came back from fingerprinting.

Patience is the key. He knew he was on his way out the door. All it took was one call and moves were being made on his behalf. "Aye my nigga, didn't your people say they were comin' to get you? You know how dis shit go my nigga, it's gon' take a minute. You gotta chill. You making me dizzy with all that damn pacing. This lil' ass box ain't but so big, ya dig?

"You right! Shit just been so crazy on my end lately. I swear a nigga don't know who to believe. I just saw a nigga from my squad riding out with my ol' lady and this was after I got to fighting with another nigga on my team."

"Shit, it looks to me like you playin' for the wrong team my nigga. I got a bunch of niggas with me, but they family. They'll die for me and I'll kill for them. You might need to leave your team and get you a family. At least with family, the last thing you have to worry about is loyalty." Head took the red bandana out of his pocket and wiped the beads of perspiration from his forehead.

Dent looked at him as he listened intently. However, he wondered to himself, it's cold as hell in here, "why is this man sweating?"

He got up from the bench, walked over to the payphone, and rapidly dialed a number. "Yo, aye lil' ma, everything come back solid? Cool, cool, cool. I need you to call 'em back and put in a card for my people." Head looked over to Dent and asked his government name.

"Antonio Smith." Dent watched as Head continued his conversation on the phone. He replayed what he had just said about the team–family and loyalty. Dent thought they were a family. He and Whyte had been thick as thieves since they were in high school. Shit, he was Whyte's first friend when he came to Atlanta. He zoned out just thinking about how he wasn't where he wanted to be–how he was tired of riding Whyte's coat-tail. Even after having bought on a whole bunch of new young niggas, providing additional business, and grooming the newbies, he had never once offered to put him on.

The steel door clicked loudly as the deputy walked in to get Head; he had just hung up the phone. He was being released. "I'm about to say something you probably ain't heard in a while. You got to fuck with who fucks with you. If a person ain't for you, they're against you. You should be out in a 'lil while. I'll have a car out front waiting on you. I think it's time you choose to ride with somebody else." He wiped his head again with his bandana, pulled up his black Dickie pants on his waist, then walked out the door behind the deputy.

As the door was closing, Dent asked what kind of car should he be looking for.

"Whateva it is, it'll be red and expensive. Everything red–always, everything expensive–always." Head said barely moving his lips.

The door clicked loudly. Dent laid down on the bench with his hands under his head and closed his eyes.

Chapter 11: A Little Break From The Monotony

Chaney hadn't talked to Dude much since he had been out in L.A. The anonymous calls had stopped but they left her mind scrambled. She really didn't know what to think. She did her best to continue with her normal day-to-day routines. She would go and open up the studio, let in the cleaning crew, go into her office, and return calls. After reading all the blogs, she would step out for lunch, go shopping sometimes, then return to the office. It was times like this that she missed her old life—when she had girlfriends that did lunch and dinner dates, went shopping together, and took trips to the spa. Presently, her entire life revolved around Dude. She missed the friends she had before she and Dude had gotten together.

They had been together less than ninety days when they got married at Fulton County Court. She didn't have any friends or family with her on that day. Within their first two months of dating, Dude had coerced her into alienating everyone that was in her life before him. All her friends believed there was something wrong with him. He wanted Chaney around him every minute of the day.

That's how she ended up working with him at his newly opened studio. The first night she spent with him, he persuaded her to quit her job at the strip club. Although she never liked displaying her body for money, that's what she had to do to afford the nice lifestyle she had grown accustomed to. Not to mention the fact that she had to take care of her family as well.

Chaney second-guessed herself in everything she did, even about Dude. She rolled with it because that was part of her personality; she always had doubts about everything. Three years later, here she was. She was aware that her gut was telling her something. She should have paid attention.

The surveillance system notified her via her computer that someone had pulled into the parking lot. She hit a few keys and was able to see Dude's best friend, who was also one of his major investors, getting out of a white Dodge Challenger SRT8. He was alone. Usually, when he came to the studio, he was either bringing someone in to do a session or was booking a session for someone. She figured he wasn't aware that Dude was still out-of-town, attempting to secure a major distribution deal for Steady Mobbing ENT.

Whyte walked into the studio and came straight to her office. He sat down in the chair facing her desk. She had never been alone in his presence. For that reason, Chaney attempted to act as though she was busy on the computer. He sat quietly for at least a minute. Chaney continued to type away. His being there was suffocating her. His Bond No. 9 cologne invaded her senses. Briefly, she stopped typing and reached for the cup of Chai Tea that she had gotten from Starbucks on her way in.

He cleared his throat. "Just stopped by to check on things. How is everything going? I know Dude has never been gone this long. Hopefully, he'll come back with some good news. We've saturated the market with mix tapes. Our artists are doing well on the radio and booking shows outside of Atlanta. We have Goldie headlining the grand opening of Luxurious next week. You really know your stuff. Did you go to school for business or marketing?"

"No, I didn't attend school for anything. I barely got my GED. However, I've been thinking of enrolling into some classes. I seem to have a knack for this and a lot of time on my hands." Chaney's voice had dropped an octave. It was something about this man that made her nervous, but in a good way.

"Yeah, you should. You can go to school online and would never have to step foot in a classroom. If you were to put some education behind the experience you already have, you could become a beast in this business. I've seen what you've done already." Whyte wouldn't have ever known that Dude's wife didn't have a formal education. She was definitely business savvy.

"I think I'll research some schools today. Thank you. Dude never encourages me to do anything that isn't directly centered around him. I appreciate the fact that you looked pass him and saw that I'm the one that's really doing all the work. It feels good to be acknowledged." Chaney felt herself blushing. She wanted him out of her office as soon as possible.

"Well, at least you're paid generously." Whyte knew he was treading lightly. He got up from his chair and looked at her closely. He knew Dude was continually cheating on her but couldn't comprehend why. She was remarkably beautiful and genuinely intelligent. She was self-taught. However, he was on the outside looking in. You never know what goes on behind closed doors.

Dude walked in with his duffle bag on his shoulder and shopping bags in both hands. "I'm sorry, did I interrupt something." His voice was dripping with sarcasm.

"Welcome back big homie." When he put his bags down on the floor in front of Chaney's desk, Whyte gave Dude a brotherly hug.

"Some good things happened out in L.A. We should be hearing something soon. I had meeting-after-meeting with all the shot callers. They love Goldie's new mixed tape. I wish we had already released it so that it could have had some spins. But that's okay. They loved the content. Even though we don't have Goldie under contract, I told them we did because a few of the A&R people were acting like they were ready to sign him." Dude walked around and stood behind his wife's chair and massaged her shoulders.

"Actually, that's what I came over here for. I have some people at the radio station that are ready to drop the mixed tape over the weekend. We need to go ahead and put it out while all the artists that are featured on it are still hot. That way, it'll have time to generate a little buzz before the grand opening performance that he's doing."

"Okay cool, I just need to call the graphic artist to see if they have the cover art ready, then it's a go." Dude said as he massaged his wife's extra-tense shoulders.

"Just get me a copy of the CD. There's no need to worry about the cover yet. Make sure you have it ready by the weekend. We should go ahead and let them make the broadcast. So that when the DJs play the songs on the radio, the mixed tape release will go hand-in-hand with the grand opening of Luxurious. I need to see if they can do an interview too. Goldie can invite the listeners to the party at Luxurious." Whyte had discovered Goldie and loved the way he rapped. He was a storyteller–a true lyricist that painted pictures with words.

Chaney was busy at her desk taking notes. Anyway, she knew she'd be doing all the work. She merely allowed Dude to bask in all the glory. Having already contacted the graphic artist, there were three cover proofs on her computer that she wanted to collaborate with Goldie on. The CDs had been delivered. She had already contacted all of the mix tape download websites as well as the radio Deejays.

"Okay, I'm outta here. I'm about to drop this CD off to my boy, then make my rounds. You two take care." Whyte made direct eye contact with Chaney; he recognized an emptiness there. He was so happy he didn't see that look when he gazed into his wife's eyes. He exited the studio then pulled out his cell phone to call Chrissy. He played in the streets because that's what a street nigga did. However, he never neglected his wife.

"He seems pretty cool. I've never talked to him before. He has connections all over doesn't he?" Chaney stated as she attempted to act busy by checking her email. She didn't even want to look Dude in his eyes after the phone calls that she'd received during his absence.

"The least he could do was put the CD in the hands of a few of the right people. I'm doing all of the real work." Dude stated as if he had an attitude because she'd said something nice about his friend.

Chaney didn't feel like arguing. Therefore, she kept pecking away at the keys on her iMac computer. She went ahead and sent the three proofs of the cover to both Goldie and Dude, and then started back reading the blogs. She was hoping he would get the hint and exit her office.

He leaned over, picked up the two shopping bags, and put them on the edge of her desk. "You know I couldn't go all the way to L.A. and not bring my favorite girl some exclusive shit back from Rodeo Drive. You gon' be the flyest motherfucker at the Luxurious grand opening party."

When he said Rodeo Drive, all Chaney saw was red. Her cheeks got flushed and her ears burned as if they were on fire. Tears welled up in her eyes. She really wanted to throw the bags on the floor, take her giant crystal peach paperweight, and beat his gay ass with it. As he pulled out shoes, dresses, and a Chanel bag that she had been wanting since Christmas, she did her best to withhold the fury and tears. "All of this is for me? What did I do to deserve this?" It would take more than some shoes, dresses, and handbags. She thought to herself. She didn't care if they were from the top designers in the world. She hurt, so he was going to hurt.

Chapter 12: Whole Pie

When Money got to the barbershop, a few people were already there. He sat down on the sofa next to Puncho who was shaking his leg nervously. Reaching over and placing his hand on his knee, he said "calm down my nigga. You on edge, you need me to roll up one?"

"Naw bruh, I stopped smoking when I got married. I'm trying to set the best example for my son. Although I've never smoked around him, I know he probably smells that shit on me. Only strong for the strong." Puncho just wanted this little impromptu meeting to be over with so that he could hurry up and get back to the hospital to be with Tameka.

Whyte sat in the barber's chair in silence, spinning it in semi circles. It appeared as though so much shit had unexpectedly happened right under his nose and he just wanted to get to the bottom of it. Goldie and Dude walked in talking to one another. They sat down in the chairs on opposite sides of Whyte. "Where's J?" He asked Goldie.

Goldie held his head down as he blushed. "She's on her way. She just dropped the kids off at home."

"Don't think I ain't heard about y'all. Just be careful lil' one. Both of y'all got some crazies on your hands with Raquel and Dent." Whyte said as he chewed on the toothpick and continued to spin back and forth. He was certain that some shit with their exes would be hitting the fan soon. Nonetheless, he couldn't prevent them from being together–they're grown. Both of them were good people who happened to be coupled up with some fucked up individuals. In reality, they needed one another.

Jordyn ran into the barbershop looking like a little girl with her hair pulled up into a high bun on her head. No make up, just some gloss on her lips. She was dressed in her usual–Christian Louboutin sneakers, jeans, and a wife beater. She pulled a wooden stool to the center of the shop where everyone was congregated. Looking around, Jordyn hoped they were the only ones attending the meeting. Due to the fiasco that occurred the last time they met, she was tired of the bullshit. However, she kept her thoughts to herself.

"Lock the door lil' one and pull the blinds." Whyte told Goldie.

Goldie did as he was told, all the while stealing glances at Jordyn. He smirked, but was beaming internally. She was like a work of art, and she was his. It was hard for him to contain his excitement. He wanted her to come and sit next to him, but he knew it wasn't professional. They were in a business meeting and she was his superior in the organization.

"Okay, let's get down to business. There's some shit going on, and it's getting worse by the day. We need to be a cohesive unit. We have the grand opening next week. I'm sure since everything else seems to be getting leaked, our affiliations with Luxurious will also be out soon. Each person that's present needs to be here. Both Julio and Pick got with me after the debacle at the club. I'm cutting back and closing doors. From this point on, everyone doesn't need to know what's happening with us. There's a betrayer amongst us. For that reason, what I'm saying from this day forth stays within the confines of those of us in this room. Your significant other, your baby mommas, baby daddy's, barbers, hairdressers, plumbers, landscapers, other workers, or partners will not be privy to our discussions or meetings. At the last gathering, I had started to talk about the gangs. Well, one in particular is coming for our piece of the pie.

I'm going to be honest. It's not a piece of the pie. We got the whole pie right now; we're eating around here. It's difficult to fade to black when you're making moves in the city like we are. Even if we don't want the attention, we're gonna get it. We can't help that big homie." Goldie said to his mentor, Whyte.

"You flooded the city with some of the purest dope it's seen since Gigi's been gon'. Atlanta's been missin' that shit. Not to mention the strongest kush and mollies. We're a force to be reckoned with. No one in the city is gettin' it like us—nobody." Jordyn said to Whyte.

"Unfortunately, there're some folks that don't like that and they want to reckon with this force. This California nigga, who bangs Blood, is trynna shake some shit up. He's set-up a house in the West End, down the street from our trap. He has another one in the Bluff, down the block from ours. Then, somebody told me he has one around the corner from your spot J'. He's a big black nigga with a baldhead and tattoos everywhere. His name is Head." Whyte rubbed his hands together as he looked around at his team.

"He must be down the street from the studio 'cause I got my shit covered in the new spot. It ain't shit shakin' 'round there that I don't know about. I know when the ice cream man pulls on the street; I know when the Sunday papers are delivered. I'm straight on my end," Jordyn said confidently.

"Puncho, why don't we know anything about this nigga, Head? That's your job. If he's making moves like that, he couldn't have slipped under your radar. Talk to us. What have you heard about this gang bangin' nigga?" Dude asked while staring at Puncho through his dark shades.

"Puncho, Puncho! You don't hear us talking to you?" Jordyn shouted to get her friend's attention–calling him and snapping her fingers in his face. He was daydreaming and picking his fingernails; he appeared to be a million miles away.

"Huh? What did you say J? My bad. My mind is still at the hospital with Meka. She was in an accident earlier."

"She was in an accident; is she alright? What the hell are you doing here then? Where's Londyn? Do you need me to do anything?" Jordyn's voice was filled with concern as she looked at her friend and saw the worry in his face.

"She was in and out when I left. The judge is there with her now and Londyn is with the neighbors." As soon as he finished his sentence, he looked over at Whyte to see if he was the least bit concerned. His facial expression hadn't changed one bit.

Jordyn became outraged. This man's wife is in the hospital, his son is with a neighbor, and he was dragged to this meeting to talk about a nigga that no one has heard about. This shit could've been done over the telephone. "Come on now Whyte. Does he really need to be here? For God's sake, the man's wife was just in a car accident."

Although he and Jordyn were close–she was like a sister to him. She was still a subordinate; she worked for him. He wouldn't allow her to talk to him like that in front of the other workers. "J,' calm yo lil' ass down. This ain't Dent you're talking to. I know this man's wife has been in an accident. I also know I'm runnin' a multi-million dollar operation that's in jeopardy. And it could be because he's not doing his job. This is business, not personal. He's not a part of this organization because he's one of my closest friends. If that were the case, Dent would've been in. He's a part of this business because he's a police officer with the City of Atlanta. We needed eyes and ears on the inside to help keep us two steps ahead of the game. It's been bought to my attention that we're way behind."

Puncho had heard about Head a while back. But he didn't think he was making noise like that. He was only selling kush. Head worked in the downtown area, which included Grady Homes, Auburn Avenue, Capitol Homes, and the Fourth Ward. That really wasn't their territory even though a lot of the niggas from that area copped worked from them. They were more so Westside and Southside. If Head was indeed making moves like that, perhaps he had somebody on the inside also. Puncho inhaled loudly. He didn't like to be chastised like a child and now wasn't the time. He knew he needed to put his ear to the streets more. However, he had just gotten his promotion to detective, was now married, and still had his program at the recreation center which he attended daily. He was bogged down. He tried to keep his business separate from his personal, but it seemed like they were both getting the best of him. At the end of the day, he wasn't doing enough. Maybe, what he really needed to do was step back.

"I'll look into it first thing tomorrow, but right now my wife and son needs me." Puncho stood up and walked out of the barbershop, leaving everybody in silence.

"That nigga need to get out his feelings and get on his job. He's fucking up majorly." Dude said to no one in particular.

"Like you know anything about feelings. You leave your wife for weeks at a time and won't even allow her to have friends. Yeah, he should really listen to you when it comes to his home life." Jordyn said to Dude. She recalled seeing Dude's wife in Phipps Plaza by herself one time–looking so sad. Jordyn mentioned it to Dude, telling him that she looked like she had lost her best friend. His reply was, he was not only her best friend, but he was her only friend. It was then that Jordyn knew that Dude was really thrown off.

"Well, if that's all, I think I'mma head over to the studio to put in some work." Goldie stood and gave Money and Dude some dap. He walked over and hugged Whyte. When he got to Jordyn, he kissed her on the forehead.

"Aren't y'all the fucking cutest? You ready for our big day next week lil' homie. It's only up from that day on." Money said as he stood to walk out with Goldie.

"Money, I need you to ride with me somewhere." Whyte got up to join them as they stood at the door.

The barbershop was quiet, only Jordyn and Dude remained. Dude moved to the barber's chair where Whyte had been sitting. Jordyn assumed he was staying behind to get a cut. She walked to the door without saying goodbye to Dude.

"That's why we'll never have a bitch in the White House. Y'all motherfuckers are too emotional." Dude said as he spun around in the barber's chair.

"That's good to know. I don't think the country could survive with somebody like you in the Oval Office— bitch ass nigga." Jordyn exited, slamming the door behind her so that it banged loudly.

Chapter 13: I Ain't Mad At Ya

Jonathan watched Tameka as she paced back and forth between their bedroom and her walk-in closet. Today was to be her first day back to work since the car accident. He had tried his best to remain the same but was currently at war within himself. He realized it was probably showing. He had been working so hard to keep his other life a secret. However, Tameka was living a double life herself. The conversation he overheard between Tameka and the judge on the night of her accident replayed over-and-over in his head. He really didn't know how to feel.

"You didn't even come to check on me! I was on the phone with you. You heard the collision but didn't even come downstairs! How am I supposed to feel about that? I could have died Janet. That police car tore the entire front-end of my car off. I could've died." Tameka *wept quietly to herself.*

Just as Jonathan was reaching to open the door, the judge began to speak. "We had just made love. I had ordered you dinner from your favorite restaurant, given you the Tiffany diamond earrings just because. Yet, you were rushing to leave me by myself to go home to him. I was hurt. It's like no matter what I do to prove my love for you, you give me your ass to kiss."

"Giving you my ass to kiss; giving you my ass to kiss! Come on now, I'm trying as hard as possible. We were supposed to end this a long time ago. I shouldn't have continued this with you after my wedding. Nevertheless, I did because I love you. I love you for always being there for me and guiding me. But I don't love you like you want me to. Janet, you were with your husband for twenty-five years. Don't you think you deserve more than someone fucking you because they feel like they're obligated to?

This is bigger than just you and me. I have a son who needed a father. Even though I wasn't out looking for one. I didn't go looking for Jonathan, he was sent to me by God. Every time I'm with you, I'm breaking the covenant that I made with God who sent me this man, who's not only a great father to my son, but a great husband as well. I can't keep doing this." Tameka lay in the hospital bed breathless and tired. She didn't feel like arguing. However, the judge not coming to check on her after the accident was the straw that broke the camel's back with them.

"I can make it up to you! What do you want? I can get you the new Lexus that just came out, or what about that BMW X6? I think you'll look good in that. Just please don't leave me. You're all I have." Janet pleaded with Tameka through tears.

"Judge, the insurance will pay for the car. I'm pretty sure that I have a lawsuit coming. The police were speeding and didn't have flashers on. My husband and I both make a decent enough salary to be able to afford a nice vehicle. I will no longer take gifts from you." Tameka finished the conversation, then rolled over onto her side—turning away from the judge.

"Please, don't leave me. We can't end like this. I love you Tameka." The judge cried loudly.

Tameka continued to lay on her side and refused to face the judge again. *"I'm not leaving you. However, we will no longer have a sexual relationship. Come hell or high water, I will be faithful to my husband. We'll pretend that late night in your office five years ago never occurred. You will continue to be my mentor and friend, nothing more. Goodnight judge."*

"Baby, how does my scar look?" Tameka asked Jonathan as she walked toward him in a snug fitting gray, pin striped dress.

He was snapped out of his trance. "It's healing very nicely. You can't tell you were in an accident two weeks ago and had glass in your head. I'm happy you'll be ready for the grand opening tomorrow." He ruffled her hair a bit to try to get it like it was before he looked at her healing scar.

I've got court today. Therefore, I'll be in and out but will probably get home before you. Dinner will be ready, whether I cook it or not. I already have our outfits for tomorrow. It'll be great to see Whyte. I haven't seen him much since our wedding." Tameka slipped into her shoes and left the bedroom.

Jonathan watched his beautiful wife walk toward the front door. He knew then and there that he couldn't do anything about what had occurred between the judge and Tameka. He witnessed his wife put the judge in her place and end the affair. Because of that, he promised to make the rest of their lives the best of their lives, and forgive her for her transgressions. "The rental car has to go back Saturday morning. We need to go to the car lot and look at some cars for you. Do you have anything in mind?"

"Yes, I like the Acura ZDX. Do you think we can afford that one?" Tameka pressed her weight into her husband and wrapped one arm around him as she stroked her hands through the hair at the nape of his neck. She leaned in to softly peck his lips; she did this over and over.

Jonathan relaxed under her weight, leaned against the wall, and wrapped his arms around her. The next time she pecked his lips, he took her bottom lip in between his. He had missed his wife, and especially missed this. Pulling her dress up, he caressed her round ass. She continued to kiss him, slipping her tongue into his mouth. A moan escaped as soon as their tongues began to assault one another's.

Tameka started to grind up against her husband's erection. She lifted her arm over her head and looked at her Cartier watch. It was only 7:25 a.m.; she had time. Pulling her dress over her head in one swift motion, she stood before her husband in the middle of the living room in her underwear. She thought he would escort her to the bedroom, but didn't.

Jonathan bent her over the blue leather sofa, and pulled down her lace panties with force. He didn't even pull his pants down; he just unzipped his fly and released his penis. Before thrusting himself inside of her vagina with force, he rubbed it back and forth over her wetness.

Her breath caught with his first thrust as he moaned loudly. It seemed like she hadn't felt her husband wandering her walls in such a long time. Tameka pushed back against him and matched his stroke. As he slammed into her repeatedly, she reached beneath her and began to massage his balls. The orgasm built up inside of her. Just as she was about to ride its first wave, her husband wrapped his hands around her neck and applied pressure.

As he slammed into her repeatedly, he imagined her fucking the judge, and his anger simmered to the top. He grabbed her around her neck and pounded his penis in and out of her while his balls smashed against her clitoris. His hips rammed into her with the force of a freight train. He heard the moans she was making. They didn't sound like her usual moans. He knew he was hurting her; he wanted to hurt her. She had been unfaithful to him. Tameka started to orgasm; he continued to apply pressure to her neck. Her walls tightened around him as he exploded inside of her.

Tameka stood up and turned around to look at her husband. "Damn baby, you just gave it to me like you were mad at me." She pulled her panties up, retrieved her dress, and headed to the bathroom.

Jonathan put his penis back inside of his pants and said silently to her retreating back, "I am."

Chapter 14: Playing Crazy

Jordyn pulled into the BP gas station on Bankhead and Bolton Road. It was unbelievable to her that there weren't any junkies lurking outside. She looked at the dark clouds that loomed in the sky and thought the pending rain had apparently scared them away. She hated pumping her own gas. In order to pay at the pump, she reached into her bag to fish out a credit card and realized she had left her wallet at home. After she'd received the call from Lucky and Goldie, she was rushing to leave the house. She intended to carry the new Chanel bag that Goldie had bought her from the mall when they went shopping for the grand opening. When she was changing purses, she must've forgotten to put her wallet inside.

Thank God she never left home without a bankroll. Reaching into her console, she retrieved a wad of money which was held together with two rubber bands. Jordyn peeled off five, twenty-dollar bills and walked inside the store. She ended up grabbing two Red Bulls and a bag of hot Cheetos. When she got to the register, she decided to play the kids' birthday and purchase a few Georgia Lottery scratch-offs. A guy she grew up with walked in and they started conversing.

As Jordyn walked out of the door, she heard tires screeching. Right away, she looked at her truck and noticed that her windshield was caved in. She sprinted to pump number four, where her truck was parked. Completely devastated, she stood there looking at her truck. She opened the driver's side door to acquire her cell phone but realized her purse was missing. There was a humongous red brick lying on her dashboard. Her childhood friend walked up behind her. "I know that bitch, Raquel didn't just bust your windshield?"

Instantaneously, Jordyn saw red as soon as she heard Goldie's baby mama's name mentioned. "Oh, that's who did this shit! That bitch grabbed my purse too. Let me see your phone right quick. My insurance will cover my windshield, but Goldie just bought me that bag."

He observed her tapping her feet impatiently as he listened to Goldie on the other end of the phone. He was in the hood everyday. Therefore, he had heard all the talk about Jordyn hooking up with Goldie. Personally, he thought it was a good look. He knew Goldie was a great nigga compared to her baby daddy, Dent. He had grown up with Dent. That nigga had been slimy since they were youngins.

She stood there listening to everything Goldie was saying. Despite the fact that her windshield was caved in, she smiled. He told her he would take care of it and she believed him. Jordyn handed her homeboy back his cell phone. He stood there with her in silence.

Just as he was sticking it in the pocket of his camouflaged cargo pants, the phone rang. He looked at the unfamiliar number and answered it. "Yo, what up?" His face twisted into a grimace as he heard the voice on the other end. It was Raquel.

"Damn my nigga, which one you working? You fucking with that bitch Jordyn too? What happened to loyalty? I'll make sure you don't get any money in the hood. Chink, you can't play both sides of the fence. I know you ran your big ass in there and told her it was me that did that to her truck, 'cause Goldie just called me. I don't know why she thinks she's untouchable. I've been sparing her ass. Fuck dat bitch, fuck you, and fuck Goldie too." Raquel said into the phone.

Jordyn watched as Chink threw his phone to the ground. His anger had turned his usually pale face into a light pink color; and his nostrils flared as he balled his fists up at his sides.

"I'mma ring that lil' bitch's neck. She ain't the mother of my kids. I'm gonna pain her lil' ass. I might go to jail for what I'm gon' do to that lil' thieving bitch. She talking big shit, but she threatening the wrong one. I ain't did shit but I'm about to give her a reason to threaten a muthafucka." Chink's temple jumped as he gritted his teeth to control his anger.

Chink was at least six feet, five inches. Even though he was tall, Jordyn definitely looked like a dwarf standing next to him. He weighed at least three hundred pounds. In high school, he was an All-Star football player. During his last year in college, he killed the man who had molested his little sister, and went to prison for ten years. His attitude about everything was fuck it and everybody knew it. No one wanted Chink to be mad at them because since he'd gotten locked up on that one body, he knew how to move. At this point, there was no telling what his body count was. The police would bring him in on shit all the time but he always got away scot-free. His hands were never found dirty.

Goldie pulled up in his Yukon Denali followed by a tow truck. Without delay, he jumped out, went straight to Jordyn, and embraced her fully. He pulled away from her, smoothed her hair back from her forehead, kissed it, and looked down at her. "You good, lil' mama?"

He had calmed her over the phone. Jordyn wanted to get in her truck–caved in windshield and all–and go shoot Etheridge up. His being by her side, made her feel as though she was under a spell. She didn't want to let him go. Things seemed too good to be true with him. Hence, she figured the shit they had going on with Raquel was the dose of reality that proved they weren't living in a fairy tale.

Goldie thought he had straightened Raquel out. Every time she asked him for something, he gave it to her. He tried his best to keep the peace. Jordyn was good for him. She was what he needed in his life. Raquel was like dead weight. Even though he had the plug with Whyte, she kept him with so much bullshit on his mind that he couldn't even think straight without being geeked on the kush or the lean. He still smoked and sipped every now and then. However, he noticed since he'd been with Jordyn, he had cut down on it; he didn't need it. His baby momma was the one that was getting on his nerves. Goldie pulled away from Jordyn, turned around, and greeted Chink. "Chink my nigga, I appreciate you staying here with wifey. Raquel can't stand to see a nigga happy. Last week, I bought that bitch a new Honda Crosstour when I bought my truck. I didn't want her to think I'm on that, I'm not fucking with my kids campaign because I have a new family.

"Man, shawty crazy–always has been. Raquel gets that from her mama. That's why her ass been in Etheridge all her life. She doesn't want anything other than to be your girl and a Westside celebrity. You need to try to get your kids. Man, shawty ain't wrapped tight. I know you don't want them to be a product of that shit." Chink said, as he got ready to walk away from them.

Goldie reached into his pocket and pulled out a bankroll. He peeled off ten crisp one hundred dollar bills. "Raquel playin' crazy. Here you go my nigga, I appreciate you looking out."

"Naw, I'm good my G'. Me and Jay go back to the sandbox. I was gon' make sure she was straight regardless. I'll holla at y'all. Let me catch this mall; I need a new phone." Chink looked at his Galaxy Note on the concrete in a million pieces and walked away.

Jordyn snatched the money from Goldie and ran behind Chink as he was getting into his black on black Impala SS. The car cranked up with a roar. You could tell he had done something to the motor because it growled like a monster. He rolled the black, tinted window down. The kush smoke hit her dead in the face. Instantly, she knew it was from her pack. She reached in and placed the folded bills in his lap. "We're not paying you for staying here with me. Take this and buy a new phone with it. That shit's smokin' ain't it? Come get you a bag of it tomorrow after three. If I'm not there, Lucky will make sure you're straight. Somehow, you're always there to bail me out." She leaned over and kissed him on his chubby check, then turned around and jogged back to Goldie's side. She remembered Chink was the reason that Dent got shot in the foot instead of in the chest. He had grabbed the gun as it was going off. Jordyn's aim was on point to kill Dent that rainy night.

Chapter 15: Holding it Together

Mercedes discovered she did indeed have cancer the day after her biopsy. Nevertheless, her recent prognosis wasn't going to stop her from working hard for all of her clients, new and previous–to get them ready for one of the biggest grand openings that Atlanta had seen in years. Cancer was not going to dim the light in her husband's eyes as he made last minute preparations for everyone in the world to see how his hard work had paid off. She didn't tell a soul. The only people that knew were her, Deja, the doctor who performed her test, and the individuals at the newly-built cancer center at Emory Hospital. She began chemotherapy right away. Money was so busy with his stuff that he didn't pay her unexplained absences any mind. He figured she was equally as busy with her work.

As the doorbell rang, she was walking to her glass and chrome worktable. She wondered who it was; she didn't recall the concierge ringing her. Then again, she was in the shower. Mercedes padded across the plush carpet with one towel on her head and another one wrapped around her. As she peered through the peephole, Deja was standing there out of her doctor's attire. Ever since her prognosis, she had been on her like white on rice.

"What you doing girly? Has my dress come yet?" Deja walked in and plopped down on the white leather chaise lounge.

"You out of your rabid ass mind coming in here plopping down on my furniture like it's a damn bean bag." Mercedes took the towel from her head and ruffled it to dry her hair.

"I'm so excited for the grand opening. Honey, I haven't been to a club since I graduated from med school." Deja stood and danced to imaginary music–dropping it low and snapping her fingers.

"Whenever I do go out, it's for work. I haven't been able to just kick it. Regrettably, I won't be able to kick it at the grand opening either. I'm not complaining. I love what I do and work is sure keeping my mind off of the big C." Mercedes sat down on the sofa, and placed the towel from her head in her lap. It was covered with her jet-black hair. A loud scream emitted from her as tears rolled down her face. She sat staring at the towel.

Deja knelt beside Mercedes on the floor, grabbed her friend, and hugged her firmly. It's going to be okay. You will lose hair with chemo. Lucky for you, growing hair has never been a problem. Are you having any other side effects from the chemo?" She rubbed her back as Mercedes kept her eyes focused on the towel while wringing her hands.

Heavyn walked in with her new Yorkshire Terrier puppy named Blue Ivy. "What's wrong mommy? Hey auntie. She knelt on the other side of her mother and put her puppy down to run around.

"I'm okay. You better pick Blue up off the floor before she finds a spot to do her business. You know what your daddy said about the first time he catches anything on this white carpet." Mercedes wiped the tears from her face and quickly folded the towel so that her daughter wouldn't see the hair.

"Why in the world did you let this man get white carpet on top of all this white ass furniture girl?" Deja asked as she looked around the immaculately decorated condo. Mercedes had an eye for styling as well because she had decorated the hell out of her home.

"Because what my king wants, he gets. When my king tells me jump, I ask how high. Not because I'm scared...but because I trust him." Mercedes inhaled deeply and leaned against the back of the sofa. She had to admit, she was worn out. Perhaps keeping the secret from Money was wearing on her more than the actual chemotherapy, she thought to herself.

Deja thought to herself that might be why she didn't have a man. She was too independent and couldn't bring herself to submit to a man to save her life.

"Well, this princess needs to go get ready for the slumber party?" Heavyn stood up and picked up her puppy.

"Wait a minute princess! You made plans for the slumber party before you got Blue Ivy. What are you going to do with her now? Your dad and I are not babysitting. We won't even be here ourselves. Why didn't I think of times like this when he told me about his idea to get you this puppy?" Mercedes was about to pick up the phone to call Money when he walked through the door with one arm filled with clothes from the dry cleaner, and his other holding onto shopping bags.

He hung the clothes up on the chrome coat rack behind the door, and dropped the bags in the foyer. It seemed like these last few weeks had gone by in a blur. He couldn't recall seeing his wife when she wasn't asleep or working on items for her clients. Money walked over to Mercedes on the sofa and gave her a long kiss. He straightened up, embraced Deja, then kissed her on the cheek. "Now Day,' I thought you stopped liking me years ago. You've started coming back around like you used to when you thought I was trying to take your best friend from you."

"Nope big brother, you know you're one of my favorite people in the world. I've been coming around to help a little bit, be nosey, spend time with my niece, and of course, get styled for one of the biggest parties this city has seen since Meech's birthday batch at the Compound." Deja was elated that her best friend had found her soul mate in Money. She was against her being with a drug dealer. However, Money constantly proved himself throughout the years. The mere fact that he signed Heavyn's birth certificate when she was born, proved he was more of a man than the one who had taken Mercedes' virginity when she was only thirteen years old. Mercedes was six months pregnant when she and Money began dating.

"Well, that's good to know. By opening my club, I've accomplished one of my biggest goals in life. The next thing on my agenda is to get you a man. I swear I'm going to do that if it's the last thing I do." Money rubbed his round belly, then reached over to smooth down Mercedes' damp hair. She pulled away from him. He looked at her sideways but didn't say anything.

Out of the corner of her eye, Deja noticed Mercedes' quick movement. She was also aware of the expression Money had on his face. "Don't find me a man…I can find my own man. I want a husband. I'm tired of being the third wheel. I wanna get married; I need to be like my favorite Kardashian, Khloe. Meet a man one day, we date, he courts me, then I'm getting married the next month. We can have the reception at the club."

Heavyn returned to the living room with a duffle bag on her shoulder and her puppy in a pink carrier.

"Who's dropping me off at my friend's house?" Her eyes lit up when she saw her father. She rushed over, put her bags down, and wrapped her arms around him.

As he picked her up slightly off the ground, Money hugged his daughter firmly. He reached into his pocket, pulled out a small folded wad of money that was held together by a money clip, removed three one hundred dollar bills, and handed them to his daughter. Next, he looked over at Deja. "I just walked in, I have so much to do today. Mercedes isn't dressed, and I don't wanna be. Can you please drop Heaven off on your way out?"

"Anything for auntie's baby. Where's my dress? My shoes were delivered yesterday and they're breathtaking." Deja felt like she was going to the prom. She couldn't wait to see the dress on her since the alterations had been made.

Mercedes stood and went in the back to get the dress. She returned with a silver garment bag and handed it to Deja. Then, she kissed Heaven on the head and thanked Deja for dropping her off.

Chapter 16: No Second Guessing

Chaney had been trying to stomach the presence of Dude since he'd been back from L.A. She had enrolled in classes at the Atlanta Metropolitan State College. For the first time in a long time, she was excited about her future. She had been working closely with Money on getting sponsorship for the grand opening party at Luxurious. Additionally, she'd scheduled him for various radio programs as well as labored with Whyte on Goldie's mixed tape release. He had built up quite a buzz. Thanks to Whyte's friend, D.J. Scream, who had debuted "Dopeman's Wife" on his nationally syndicated radio show last week, his first single was blowing up across the country.

Dude walked into the office just as she was about to leave to go meet Whyte. She had to present him with the final layout for the graphics that would be inserted with the CD. Ten thousand copies had been scheduled for delivery tomorrow. It was crunch time, Dude wanted to call the shots, but didn't want to get his hands dirty. Not one time had he asked what he could do to help. Chaney's frustration was apparent as she exhaled heavily, walked pass him, and out of the door without a word.

Dude grabbed her arm forcefully. "Bitch, what the fuck is your problem. You've been acting real lame since I got back from L.A. I don't have time for this shit. I'm not about to tip-toe around this muthafucka, and I damn sho not about to kiss your ass. If you got a problem with me, let me know."

Now was the perfect time for her to tell him everything that was on her mind. Holding all the bullshit inside made her a ticking time bomb. Chaney didn't want to keep Whyte waiting. Therefore, she sucked her teeth loudly as she looked down at her Audemars Piguet watch that Dude had purchased for her on their first anniversary. "I'm taking care of business. I don't have time to do this right now. But trust me, when I do have a second to spare, you'll definitely know what's going on with me." She snatched her arm away from Dude and walked out the door.

Dude watched his wife pull off before pulling out his phone. He had enough going on already without her bitching. To stop the blackmail, he had to figure out a way to get out of paying his former lover the one hundred thousand dollars he was requesting. He knew Chaney would be gone for a while. Therefore, he wanted to sit down and talk some sense into his lover. "Come to the studio, no one is here. We need to talk."

Goldie had been on pins and needles lately. The war that Raquel had raged against him and Jordyn was taking its toll on him. He missed seeing his two kids. This was supposed to be the happiest time in his life. He had the woman of his dreams, his career was taking off, and he was making money so fast it scared him. Reaching into his center console, he pulled out a pre-rolled blunt of kush and lit it as he headed to the studio. He thought about how Jordyn put him first and tried to make sure he was straight no matter what. He laughed to himself as he reminisced about their morning together.

Jordyn rolled over, jumped out of the bed naked, and ran into the adjoining bathroom. A few minutes later, she returned then slid back into bed with Goldie. After putting her head beneath the covers, she pulled his penis from his boxer briefs. She placed his soft penis into her mouth and proceeded to suck and lick on it loudly, until it was standing at full attention.

He tried to stretch his body a little bit but couldn't. She had him at her mercy as she sucked him into submission. If he didn't love her already, the amazing sex that she gave him twice a day was damn sure gonna make it happen. "Damn girl, what you tryna do to me?"

Jordyn removed her head from under the covers and looked into his eyes. "If you're full when you leave home, I guarantee you won't eat at them fast food restaurants."

"Girl, what you talking about? You know I hate fast food. But I will get take out from Benihana's, Longhorn's, or something like that." He said as he stretched his legs around her body.

"Nigga, I'm talking about if I satisfy your sexual appetite, then you won't be out here fucking with these little girls who be gunnin' for you." Jordyn said before putting his penis back into her mouth.

"Baby trust me, that's the last thing you have to worry about. Bring that pussy up here and give me my breakfast." Goldie said as they got into the sixty-nine position.

The first orgasm hit her like a wave crashing onto the shore. Before she and Goldie had gotten together, she had never experienced an orgasm. She was an avid reader. However, she had never read words that came close to summing-up the euphoric feeling this man had constantly given her. As the convulsions went through her body, she stopped slurping on him and bit down on her bottom lip. Never in a million years could Jordyn imagine someone so young, being so skilled sexually. Lord knows that Goldie could teach Dent a few things. She felt as if she'd been deprived these past ten years with Dent.

Goldie rolled over, quickly taking Jordyn's petite frame with him. He pinned her down as he slid inside of her in one swift movement. As his hips pumped back and forth, he kissed her passionately; the taste of both of them filled his mouth as their tongues danced the tango.

Breaking the kiss, he said, "I belong to you; you belong to me."

Those words coupled with him stroking her just right, caused another orgasm to sweep over her. Jordyn was addicted to this man; she could never get enough of him. She felt him start to go faster, pounding in and out of her. Just as she started to climax, he ejaculated his warm seed into her. Reaching up and grabbing his face, she kissed him while she wrapped her legs around his body, and clinched her vaginal walls to ensure she received every last drop of him.

"They ain't got nothing on you baby. No need for any second guessing." Goldie got up and went into the bathroom. His cell phone was ringing constantly. He glanced at it briefly on the counter before he got into the shower. It was a blocked caller. Raquel just wouldn't let up. Despite the fact that he hadn't seen his children in almost two months, she still wanted him to drop money off to her mom every week. If it weren't for Jordyn, she wouldn't get anything. However, Jordyn showed him the rationality of it all. She spoke to him like a single mother. Therefore, regardless of the hell he'd been going through with Raquel, he continued to go to Etheridge every Monday to take six hundred dollars in cash to Raquel's mom.

Jordyn knew even though Goldie wasn't talking to her about it, being away from his kids was getting the best of him. He was sleeping less than four hours a day. He was either in the trap house, the studio, with her, or helping Lucky with his studio. She was trying her best to be what he needed, but she knew he was missing a big piece of himself. Naked, she sat on the side of the bed rolling his blunts for the day out of a big Ziploc bag of kush that they kept at home. While he was having his problems with Raquel, it seemed as if Dent had disappeared from the face of the earth. Initially, she was worried that he was still locked up. She went and got her car from the impound lot and checked to see if he had been released.

She didn't want to talk about her problems with Whyte, especially after the fight at the club that night. She wanted to know if Whyte bailed him out. And if so, what did he say. Jordyn had been at such peace, that she had to question if this was the calm before the storm, or was Dent really just allowing her to go without a fight?

Goldie exited the bathroom soaking wet, wrapped in a towel. The water beaded on his dark, honey-colored skin. You could see the fine golden blonde hairs that were everywhere on his body. "You good baby? I think I'mma head over to the studio and work for a little while. I got some stuff floating around in my head that I need to get out." He went into the walk-in closet and started to get dressed.

Jordyn told Goldie that he was welcomed to move in, but he refused. He informed her that he didn't want to lay his head in another man's bed. When he did spend the night at Jordyn's house, they slept in the guest room. He had accumulated a wardrobe at her house. Although she didn't tell him, she had already begun the search for another dwelling in which both of them could feel comfortable calling home. As soon as he was finished with the promos for the mixed tape as well as the grand opening for Luxurious, she was going to tell him to try and get custody of his kids from Raquel. "I'm fine, I need to get up. I've got work to do."

Goldie let himself into the studio with his key and punched in the alarm code. He had some instrumentals playing in his ears via his Beats by Dre headphones. Dude's car was in the parking lot, but he didn't want to talk to anyone. His only objective was to get on the microphone. When he went inside, he didn't see the engineer. He walked the hall and noticed Chaney wasn't in her office. Dude's office door was ajar. He pushed the door open and what he saw made him gasp aloud.

Dude was on the desk in the buck being fucked. His legs were in the air being held by some very manly hands belonging to a man dressed as a woman with waist length blond hair. The transvestite had on red stiletto high heels and a skin-tight leopard print dress which was up above his waist.

Goldie stood in shock as the bile rose in his throat. The transvestite had clearly had some work done. His ass was perfect and he could see breasts bouncing up and down with each thrust. There was no second-guessing that this was indeed a man. Unable to hold it back any longer, he vomited. Loud enough to startle and cause them both to stop. Goldie turned around, ran down the hall, and out the door of the studio.

Chapter 17: Welcome to Atlanta

The strobe lights fluttered, illuminating the sky of downtown Atlanta. The black carpet was flooded with the "who's who" of Atlanta stopping to take pictures, hugging, and kissing. The line of luxury cars, being parked by valets attired in black and platinum tuxedos, had doubled in size as the traffic had come to a complete standstill on Peachtree Street.

Many people didn't believe it could be done. Numerous residents and businesses along this billion-dollar corridor were against opening a club on Peachtree Street again. Luckily, Money and Whyte knew people in high places. They had purchased season tickets, padded pockets, paid private school tuitions, and bankrolled braces–all to make this night possible. The dream had become reality. If only for one night, Whyte and his crew were on top of the world.

Chrissy had been on edge for the past three weeks. Seeing her husband put on the bullet proof vest underneath his Tom Ford tuxedo didn't help to relax her apprehension. He had assured her it was just a precaution. She didn't say anything. However, in her mind, she was convinced there was some underlying issue that warranted her husband wear a vest. She slipped into her Cobalt and Platinum colored Tom Ford dress while quietly praying that this night goes off without a hitch.

Whyte did his best to keep what he had heard from Puncho under wraps. In spite of this, it was extremely difficult. He wanted to go and beat Dent to death. Dent had sided with the enemy. He had joined Head and the Bloods. Whyte should've known something was wrong when he didn't hear from him after he bailed him out. He took it to mean that maybe he was attempting to get out of paying him back the bail money. He had heard that Jordyn had all of his stuff put on his mom's front steps, but that's where it ended. Since the fight in the club, he hadn't seen hide nor hair of him.

It was one thing to have enemies. Consequently, it was an entirely different ballgame when the enemy's secret weapon was one of your own. Whyte wanted to be ten steps ahead. He had hired triple security and ordered everyone to wear bulletproof vests underneath their tuxedos. He even wanted Jordyn to wear one. Of course, she couldn't do so inconspicuously. Therefore, he had two security guards, one male and one female, that were to stay by her side at all times.

There was a knock on their bedroom door. Chrissy looked over at her husband before going to open the door. It could only be Pretty, he was the only one who had access to their home like that. Pretty entered in a cobalt blue tuxedo with a platinum shirt underneath. He didn't have on a tie; his shirt was opened at the collar. "Well, aren't we just the fucking cutest? Bitch, look at you matching my fly. Hey Whyte."

"What's up with y'all matching? Baby you're supposed to be matching my fly, not his. Everybody ready, the car is downstairs waiting." Whyte had ordered a platinum colored Phantom for them. Tonight, all the associates would arrive in platinum colored cars.

Mercedes realized that even though she had only been doing chemotherapy for three weeks, she had lost weight. Any other time, she would be happy about the weight lost, but not this time. She slipped into the two-toned skintight white and platinum Alexander McQueen dress. Turning around, she looked at herself in the full-length mirror that was on the back of her closet door. The dress hugged her every curve. She had to admit, she looked fantastic. Her friend and new makeup artist to the stars, Tawana applied her makeup to perfection. Her jet-black pin curls were shining and coifed, making her face look like a porcelain doll. Frenshel Cooper at Salon Ramsey had showed out as usual. Although she was sick, Mercedes looked better than she had in years.

As his wife was walking out of the closet, Money walked into their bedroom. His breath was caught in his throat as he witnessed how gorgeous she looked. "Hey miss lady, you looking good and all, but I don't think my wife would want me to share this night with anybody but her."

She wished they were in Las Vegas right now; they could leave the grand opening and go get married. At this moment, this is how she imagined them looking. Money appeared immaculate in his all white Versace tuxedo. He wore a platinum shirt underneath. The contrast against his dark skin painted the perfect picture. Mercedes went to her husband, whose smile showed his approval of her appearance, and wrapped her arms around him. She felt the stiff hardness of the bulletproof vest. Although worried, she refrained from saying anything. This would be the last night of normalcy for them. She had told Deja earlier that she would tell Money that she had cancer first thing tomorrow.

"Baby, what do you think?" He said as they exited the building and the platinum Bugatti was sitting out front waiting on them. He opened the door for his wife, then walked around and got in. Money opened the center console and removed two large jewelry boxes. The box on top was the unmistakable Cartier Red, and the large one on the bottom was black velvet. First, he opened the top box. Lying inside was a platinum necklace with a large black diamond in the middle, surrounded by other diamonds.

Mercedes was as giddy as a child on Christmas. She loved the fact that her husband always showered her and their daughter with gifts, just because. This time, he had outdone himself with this necklace. It was amazing. She leaned over while he placed it around her neck. After she gave him a passionate kiss, she took her finger and wiped the Ka'oir platinum lipstick from her husband's lips.

"I'm done baby, I'm officially out of the streets. Tonight, is the first night of the rest of our lives." Then he opened the black velvet box and pulled out a long platinum chain with a moneybag charm on it. Written across the diamond encrusted money bag was "Ex Drug Dealer" in black diamonds. After his long talk with Whyte last night, he knew this was the best time for him to make his exit. Some shit was about to hit the fan. Presently, he has a legitimate business that's about to bring in all the money that he needs to take care of his wife and children.

They zipped through the streets of downtown Atlanta, floating on a cloud in one of the fastest cars in the world. Mercedes' hand was on her husband's knee as he drove the car like an expert. "Baby, I like this. How long do you have it for?"

"For the weekend, but I'm telling you, I could get used to this. I fell in love as soon as I got in it. But I don't think I would pay almost two million for a car no matter how much money we had." He said as they turned onto Peachtree Street. Tears welled up in Money's eyes as he saw how the street was illuminated, and packed with wall-to-wall traffic. Bodies were on both sides of the street. People were either entering the club, or attempting to see who the individuals were that were gaining admission.

Puncho's black tuxedo jacket and platinum pants looked great with what his wife had on. They were dressed alike. Tameka had on a black iridescent motor cycle jacket that was studded with Swarovski crystals, and platinum iridescent tailored pants–both made by Front Row. Her jet black hair was slicked down to her head. She had on the Tiffany earrings that the judge had gifted her. This was her first time wearing them. Thinking her husband wouldn't notice, she snuck them on.

"Since we've been married, we have never been to a club together. This is going to be our first club date. Please don't let your temper get the best of you tonight Detective Harper. If you have a woman and nobody's looking at her, then you don't really have yourself anything, do you?" Tameka didn't want her husband to go jumping down anyone's throat if they approached her in this environment.

"I'll keep calm. I'm a policeman baby. If this wasn't the biggest night in my two closest friends' life, we still wouldn't be going to a club together." While he knew his wife's secret, she still didn't know his. He was the inside man for one of the largest drug dealers in the city.

The platinum Challenger SRT8 had been delivered to their townhouse at noon. Puncho immediately called Whyte to talk about driving the car and how it would make him look. "Man you know I got to keep a low-key profile. I can't be coming to the grand opening driving this expensive ass car." He told his best friend over the phone while the deliveryman was still at his door.

"Man, calm down lil' bro. That ain't expensive, it's just an SRT8. I'm coming in a Phantom, Money's coming in a Bugatti, and Julio actually bought a new platinum Bentley Coupe. Jordyn and Money are pullin' up in a platinum Porsche 911, and you know Dude's ol' extra ass gotta come with a Maybach. We're showing out tonight. Trust me, compared to us, the Challenger is modest." Whyte assured his friend.

After Whyte put it in perspective, he was okay. The Challenger was a drop in the bucket compared to what the other members of the organization were showing up in.

"It was so nice of Whyte to get us a car, especially for the grand opening. You know your best friend is really a class act." Tameka said to her husband as she slid into the passenger seat of the sports car.

"You know Whyte always has to do it big, and so does Money. There's no telling what we're about to witness when we pull up at the club. Either way, I know it's going to be amazing." Puncho headed toward downtown leaving their townhouse in the SWATS, and driving the car at top speeds.

Jordyn's petite frame filled the ice blue, floor length, skintight, backless BCBG Max Azria dress. She could barely move. It felt like she had literally been poured into the dress. Goldie had selected it for her. Her hair had been pressed out. It hung just above her waist on her bare, tattoo-filled back. She was wearing a dress, but she was damn sure not putting on any high heels. She had on some Swarovski crystal encrusted Givenchy ballet slippers. As a result of her dress nearly dragging the floor and pooling around her shoes, her feet barely showed.

Goldie walked in and instantly all the crazy thoughts that had been filling his head for the past three days–of walking in on Dude–suddenly went out the window. Tonight was going to be the best night of his life. He strolled across the floor in three giant steps and swept up the woman of his dreams into his arms. Fuck Dude's punk ass, Fuck Raquel's bitch ass. Tonight was going to be the best day of his life.

"Now where did Money's wife find you a True Religion denim tuxedo at? I've never seen anything like this baby." Jordyn gazed at Goldie with pride. He looked so good in the custom made True Religion tuxedo that he wore. He had on a screen print shirt with his mixed tape cover on it.

"She had it custom made. This is ten pairs of jeans, I think she said. This shit is fly tho, ain't it? She's the stylist for all the stars in Atlanta. I'm just happy I had the inside track to get to her. I'm sure she wouldn't have been available if I tried to get at her without Money being my people.

They walked outside and got into the Porsche 911 that Whyte had delivered to Jordyn's house earlier that afternoon. "Yep, we know for a fact it's not about what you know, it's about who you know."

Dude had been being extremely nice to his wife. Not because of all the hard work that she'd put in to help pull off this event, but because he knew the shit was about to hit the fan. He had been walking on eggshells ever since Goldie walked in on him and Gucci, his lover for the past five years.

It was bad enough that Gucci was blackmailing him. He, or rather she wouldn't leave the office that day without him handing over ten thousand dollars in cash. In Dude's mind, he intended to end the relationship with the transvestite when he married his wife. However, it seemed like Gucci went even harder after he married Chaney. Dude had to admit, he was addicted to the sex he was having with Gucci. Plus, she had him by the balls, literally. She called all the shots. He was simply a puppet on a string.

Chaney entered with a thigh length platinum dress that was form fitting, and cut so deeply in the front that you could see her belly button. The peek-a-boo dress was definitely a showstopper. She expected her husband to tell her to change into something else; she had another Platinum dress on standby in case he did. Nevertheless, he didn't. He sipped something clear from a glass as she made her way down the stairs.

Dude had to be a fool to be cheating on a woman that looked like Chaney, to be unfaithful to someone who displayed the loyalty she had, and was as smart as Chaney was. Dude knew he was a fool–an individual with a sexual hunger that was only satisfied by men who looked like women. Any man would, more than likely, be overjoyed to have a woman with half of his wife's attributes.

Chaney walked right pass her husband. Her jeweled Christian Louboutin's were clicking loudly on the marble floor in the foyer as she went outside and got into the platinum colored chauffeured Maybach. Dude got in but didn't say a word as they headed to the grand opening of Luxurious.

Chapter 18: This Life Is So Exciting

The camera flashes were going off everywhere as people took pictures and danced to D. J. Scream spinning the top hits. The elevated VIP booths, as well as the tables, were all filled to capacity. There was barely enough room to walk, much less dance. The bottle girls were walking back and forth in platinum colored, bejeweled one pieces, providing bottles of top notch liquor to people all over the club. In order to draw attention to the crew, the bottle girls held the trays high above their heads as the sparklers made receiving a bottle of alcohol even more exciting.

With the exception of Goldie, Whyte, Money, Puncho, Jordyn, Julio, and their significant others were in the "Diamond" V.I.P. area. They were sectioned off from the other VIP areas. This particular zone was elevated slightly higher and incased in glass with carved diamond patterns on it. The ladies all acted cordial to one another as their husbands introduced them. Each one complimented the other on their attire for the evening. This was actually the first black tie event they had all attended together. Nonetheless, through pillow talk with their mates, each person had heard a lot about the other.

"I hope there's someone in here that I'm attracted to tonight. All of you are coupled up." Pretty said as he joined them in VIP.

"Don't worry Pretty, my best friend is coming and she's single too." Mercedes said to the hairstylist that she had worked with on several occasions.

Jordyn overheard the conversation and leaned her head back to say: "Julio is single for the moment too. Everybody's not in relationships. Hey, I'm Jordyn." She extended her small hand to Mercedes.

"Girl, you better do better than that and give me a hug, as much as my husband is always talking about you." Mercedes held Jordyn in a warm embrace. She saw the look of shock on Deja's face just as she remembered that her oncologist had warned her to be extra careful when being around people. Their minor germs could become a major infection to her.

A smile radiated across Jordyn's face. She could see why Money was so in love with his wife after all these years. Not only was she drop-dead gorgeous, she was extremely sweet. "I feel like I know you too. Money is always talking about you. Of course, he left out the part about you being a showstopper. Girl, you got some good genes. You look like you're in your late teens."

"I tell her that every time I see her on a shoot, but I don't know what it is tonight. I guess I'm not used to seeing her in real clothes or something. You shining bright baby girl. Whatever it is, keep it up." Pretty said to Mercedes.

"I thought you would've taken your ass down there to start shopping." Chrissy said to Pretty as she walked over to where they were in conversation.

"Excuse this rude bitch, this is my other half, Chrissy. She's also Whyte's other half." Pretty smacked his lips as he introduced Chrissy to Mercedes and Jordyn.

"I'm sorry. Hey ladies. It's just that all this bitch has been talking about was coming to this party to catch him a man. Now he's sitting up here cackling with you all. I'm the one that's gonna have to hear the fallout if he doesn't get any phone numbers tonight." Chrissy said as she looked at both Jordyn and Mercedes. She thought to herself, this isn't how I pictured Jordyn. She imagined her to be a tomboy, a more masculine type. Insecurity immediately snuck in. She didn't know if she felt comfortable with her husband working so closely with a female that looked like her.

The lights started to flash on and off as D.J. Scream dropped the intro beat to Goldie's mixed tape. The crowd got hyped up then everyone faced the dark stage. Suddenly, all the lights went out in the club and the beat stopped. Fireworks erupted. On the stage, the lights came back as two white tigers, a lion, and a bear sauntered to and fro across the platform. Once again, the music played and Goldie strolled out with microphone in hand, singing his new street hit, "Westside Zoo."

"I can speak 'bout me, but I can't speak 'bout you.

I was raised in this Westside Zoo.

Trappin' Monday through Friday and the weekends too, that's how I get it in, in this Westside Zoo.

I used to ride through my hood on BMX bikes,

Now I'm serving blocks to some eastside Dykes.

(You know) Now I'm cooking it up, keep the fiends ready with that pipe.

I got it all, the hard you need, but I still keep that soft white.

I got some business executives that hit my line faithfully.

I got my nick smoking junkies that really help make me.

I got my bad bitch by my side faithfully, and then a bunch of pussy niggas that always fake to me.

But when it comes down to it, I just straight do it.

He got a couple goons wit 'em,

I got the whole Zoo wit' me.

U got some niggas that will snitch.

U got some niggas that will switch.

U got some niggas that will bitch all over a bitch.

But when it comes down to it, it's gonna be me & u.

U might have the Cali bloods but I got the Westside Zoo.

I got some lions that will roar, some tigers that will pounce.

Catch 'ur ass slippin' on Bankhead, right by the Bounce.

Got some bears wit' me, that will rip yo' ass apart. They will tear you from limb to limb, then eat your heart.

You got some niggas that will switch.

With my team it's all about the green, no red, or no blue.

We gettin' money over here in this Westside Zoo."

"Ayyyyyye, we gettin' money in this Westside Zoo!" Whyte screamed as ones, fives, and ten dollar bills rained from bags attached to the ceiling. He beamed with pride as he watched Goldie on the stage with the microphone in his hand. He had totally redone the song. What he just recited wasn't what was on the mixed tape. Nonetheless, he had to admit that it went even harder and was perfect. The crowd loved it. The chorus kept replaying as Goldie exited the stage accompanied by Lucky, Dude, and some other guys he had saw at the studio with Goldie. His performance was outstanding. The sky was definitely the limit for him.

The dim club lights came back on as the stage lights went off. Seated at the front table, right off the stage, were six men in all white tuxedos, surrounded by at least fifteen more men dressed the same. It wasn't the white tuxedo's that made them stand out. It was the red bandanas that were tied around their elbows and hanging out of their back pockets. Sitting in the middle of the table was Head, dressed in a red tuxedo with a Boston Red Sox baseball cap on and a big red B on the front. Right beside him sat Dent.

Chapter 19: The Golden Child

The adrenaline was pumping through his veins as he strolled down the stairs from the stage. After he had spoken to Whyte last night, he went into the studio that he and Lucky had been working on. Goldie had learned to take all his problems straight to the booth. This tactic was sparing a lot of people. He couldn't believe how the crowd had reacted to his remix of "Westside Zoo."

"Oh my God, baby! That was awesome!" Jordyn rushed into his arms, then started jumping up and down. The euphoric feeling she was displaying was exactly how he felt on the inside. That goes to show how strong their connection was.

"So, I guess that means you liked it." Goldie said as he wrapped his arms around her.

"Yes, I did. Baby you went in. Nobody was expecting that." Jordyn said as she looked up at the young man who had stolen her heart.

"We sure weren't expecting it. You did real good baby daddy." Raquel walked up behind them as silent as a ghost.

"Who in the hell let the street-walkers in? I meant the thieves; I meant the street-walkers that are thieves. Where's the security? Where's Whyte?" Jordyn said as she looked around to escort Raquel off the premises.

"Bitch, I don't see your momma in here. Although it does look like both of y'all just saw a ghost." Raquel said as she smacked her lips and put her hand on her hip.

Jordyn knew this was not the time nor the place. She wanted to pick up the first bottle that she saw and crack it right upside Raquel's head. Looking up into the Diamonds V.I.P. booth, she noticed that Whyte and Julio were on their way down. However, they weren't headed in her direction. She looked at Whyte and followed his intent glare and saw he was headed to the table of men in the white tuxedos. The look in Whyte's eyes told her something was about to pop off.

"Raq, go sit your ass down somewhere before I have your ass thrown out this mother fucker like Jazzy Jeff on The Fresh Prince of Bel-Air." Goldie said as he grabbed Jordyn's arm harder than he intended, so they could walk to where Whyte was headed.

"That's alright, enjoy yourself tonight. But trust and believe, tonight is the last night the both of you will be smiling and happy. God don't like ugly." Raquel said to their retreating backs.

"Well, why in the hell does he keep sparing your fugly ass then bitch?" Jordyn said before turning around, walking away, and matching Goldie's strides across the room.

A smile spread across Dent's face when he noticed his baby's mother approaching. For quite some time, he had been yearning for this moment. He couldn't wait until she saw him shining. He had stayed away for as long as he did so that he could get this very reaction out of his former crew. It was as though he had dropped off the face of the earth and was now being resurrected. As everyone else looked at him, his eyes remained on Jordyn. He had never seen her look so beautiful in his life.

"Well damn baby, not only did you bring out the animals from the zoo, but it looks like you also bought out the scum of the earth." Jordyn said as she snuggled tightly into Goldie's armpit.

"Once a disrespectful bitch, always a disrespectful bitch. You went and got yourself a young nigga that'll let you do and say whatever you want. Better him than me." Dent said as he got up from the table.

Goldie looked around and stated, "I only see one bitch right now and that's your dick-ridin' ass. I see you found a new one to bounce on. That's fine and good. Just don't disrespect my queen again my nigga. I'm not gon' put a hot one in your foot and that's a promise."

"You threatening me young nigga? This ain't what you want. You better calm down Golden Child 'cause the big homie ain't gonna be everywhere with you. Damn, I thought y'all niggas was gonna be happy to see me." Dent said sarcastically, while looking at the individuals who were once the closest thing to him.

"Nigga, you disappear like a thief in the night and think we're supposed to be all happy, happy, joy, joy to see you. You could have at least called me." Pick said to his older brother as he joined everyone else surrounding the table.

"Man, you were never worried about me. I didn't leave the city; I was right under y'all noses. No one reported me missing, but I appreciate y'all acting like you cared. Now I know what family is, in the true sense of the word. I thought y'all were my family, but I got left for dead. I'm happy some real niggas came to my rescue." Dent said as he waved his arm dramatically to point out his new crew.

"Left for dead? Nigga, the last time I heard from you, you called begging me to get you out of Rice Street and I ain't heard from you since. Oh yeah, by the way, you're welcome." Whyte was trying his best to control his temper as he clenched and unclenched his fists at his side. He wanted to punch the hell out of Dent's ass. Ever since he met him, he'd been carrying the nigga.

"What the fuck am I supposed to be thankful for? You didn't come get me. This man right here got me out and had a car waiting on me. It was this man that took me in, put me on–he plugged me in." Dent said pointing at Head, who sat quietly cheesing like a Cheshire cat.

Head was getting a kick out of all of the upheaval he had created. Because he had the upper hand on them, he was indeed, at present, the most powerful. He knew all of their secrets and had their secret weapon. Glimpsing up from the table, he nodded his head to his friend who was sitting at the bar by himself watching the show. Things were falling right into place. Tonight, Dent was going to complete his initiation and truly become family.

Jordyn locked eyes with Head. She had seen this man before. His daughter went to Southwest Christian Academy with her sister, and they were friends. She'd seen him at some of the school functions. Her little sister told her he was a single father, that it was just him and his daughter. She wondered to herself, "how are you a gang bangin', drug dealin', single father?" I guess the same way you're a drug dealin' single mother. You make shit happen.

When Dude approached, his eyes widened as soon as he saw Head seated in the middle of the table. Instantly, he felt flushed. Unbuttoning the top three buttons on his shirt, he did his best to relax. He had seen him in California when he and his lover were eating at the hotel. Chaney was standing beside him; he immediately grabbed her hand. All night, he had kept her by his side, not even allowing her to talk to the other wives. He glanced at Goldie who was staring at him. This was the first time he had been in Goldie's presence since he walked in on him. He had been calling him but he hadn't picked up. He prayed that Goldie would keep his secret. Nevertheless, he had something up his sleeve in case he wouldn't.

Whyte cleared his throat. "This is a special evening and we want all our guests to feel welcomed and accommodated. We're confident this table has felt our presence. Let's visit all the other VIP areas as well. A bottle of Louie on the house." He tapped the table and walked off with the rest of the crew accompanying him.

Money joined in, "enjoy your night gentlemen".

Goldie looked Dent in the eyes and said loudly, "now dats how bosses do it." He and Jordyn bought up the rear as the crew moved from table-to-table greeting guests and informing them of their complimentary bottle of champagne.

Head looked over at Dent. "Are you ready to officially become a member of the family? You know what you have to do. What had just transpired only added fuel to the fire."

Dent rubbed his hands together and squinted his eyes. "Yeah, I'm ready. It's about that time."

Chapter 20: Surprise, Surprise, Surprise

The grand opening turned out to be more than a success. All the visitors were gone. The crew and their significant others, as well as a few guests were in the boom-boom room recounting the night's events. Downstairs in the club, a cleaning crew was cleaning up and the bartenders were restocking the bar. D.J. Scream and his assistant were packing everything away.

"Aye, look around and see if you can find Goldie for me. I need to chop it up with him before I leave. I see him going straight to the moon. I've got to find out who his people is." D.J. Scream said to his assistant.

"Yeah, I like his style. But you know he's with Whyte and Dude. He's Steady Mobbing." The assistant said to D.J. Scream.

"I can handle Whyte, them my people. Go get Goldie." D.J. Scream placed his MacBook Pro in its case.

Jordyn sat on the edge of Money's desk with one foot dangling. Pick and Julio were shooting pool. "I damn sure wasn't expecting that. Somebody please tell me you got some kush. My nerves are shot; I need a blunt for real. I wanted to duck out the back door when I saw that clown's face. First Raquel, then him. I thought I was gon' blow a head gasket."

Hearing her say those words caused Chrissy to loosen up a bit. Even though she was dressed like a princess and was extremely beautiful, what her husband said about Jordyn was true. She really acted like one of the guys. Chrissy looked over at her husband who was sitting in a recliner rotating his thumbs–something he did when he was deep in thought.

"Okay, I'm not gonna keep y'all too long. I just wanted to take a little time to thank each and every member of this team. If you're here because you're married to a member of this crew, then I'm thanking you as well for loaning your significant other to me. This is my family. I love y'all and I wouldn't have wanted to share this night with anybody else in the world. Salute!" Money kissed his wife on the top of her head then raised his bottle of champagne.

"Congratulations my nigga. If anybody deserves this, you do. You've been on this club grind, making money for other niggas for a long time. Now it's your time to shine. Salute!" Dude raised his bottle. His wife was sitting on his lap as he sat in one of the lounge chairs. Chaney had been quiet tonight.

"If I ever wanted to see someone's dream come true, it's yours my brother. Congratulations! I hope that piece around your neck means this is officially your last night in the game." Puncho said to his long-time friend, happy that he had decided to go fully legit. His wife, Tameka held up her bottle of champagne, pointed it in his direction, and took a big gulp.

"I'm so proud of each and every one in this room. If there was ever a doubt in a motherfucker's mind about what we could do, tonight proved everybody wrong. It feel's good to be part of a winning team. My whole team balls, go N.B.A. We're going straight to the top now that all the dead weight is gone and there's no infighting. There's nothing but positive energy surrounding all of us. To all of us!" Jordyn picked up her bottle from the desk and raised it.

Goldie's emotions had been intact for the entire night. However, right now, he was overwhelmed. He raised his bottle as tears flowed from his eyes. "I wanna take this time to tell all y'all that I love you. I will lay down my life for you. Two years ago, I literally didn't have a pot to piss in or a window to throw it out of. My wardrobe consisted of one pair of Levi's and two Ralph Lauren Polo Shirts. Other than my two kids, I don't have any family. When I was able to catch a few winks, I was sleeping at different homeboys' houses. Some days, I couldn't even eat; other days, I only had ramen noodles. I used to always see this man driving around. He was a legend and I said if I ever got a chance to talk to him, I was going to ask him to teach me. And that's exactly what I did. I never told him I was homeless, or hungry. I never had my hand out; I didn't want anyone to have pity on me. Then one day, in front of the gas station, I saw him. Niggas was asking him to let 'em hold something. I spoke louder than all of them and said teach me! That day, I left the gas station with him and it's been on go ever since then." Tears fell freely from Goldie's eyes as he looked at Whyte.

"That's why whatever I got, you can have. The difference between you and them other niggas is that you knew if you learned to fish, you would never go hungry again. Them niggas wanna eat, you feed 'em, then they're coming right back to you with their hands out when they're hungry. Real…grown men want to feed themselves." Listening to Goldie, Whyte was getting emotional himself.

"I owe tonight to you; I owe my life to you. You're one of the realest men I know and I mean that in every sense of the word, from the bottom of my heart. It's nothing but love in here for you!" Goldie pounded on his chest and pointed his fist at Whyte.

"Man, you 'bout to make me cry. That's enough of that. Tonight, is the first of many successful, legit nights for us. We do what we do as a means to an end. We're not hustling this shit forever. That isn't in my plan for myself; and it isn't in my plan for you either. Pretty soon, all of us will be exactly where we wanna be. But in the meantime, I got everybody a little something to help get him or her get there a little sooner. Two of you already received yours. The rest of you will have deliveries before the week is out. Goldie, the 911, that's yours. Puncho, the Challenger, that's yours. Everyone else, be on the look-out for your surprises. Salute!" Whyte raised his glass. This was the first time he had done anything this extravagant for his team. However, after seeing how Dent had turned against them, it let him know his gifts were only solidifying the crew's allegiance to him and showing his appreciation.

Goldie started jumping up and down, rushed over, and hugged Whyte like he was a big kid.

Meanwhile, Dude sat with his wife on his lap watching how Whyte and Goldie were fawning over one another. Goldie didn't thank him one time for assisting him with his career. It was his studio and his record label. He had made Goldie the face of Steady Mobbing ENT. His lyrics and speech seemed to mock him. He needed to do something to shut him up.

D.J. Scream's assistant knocked on the door and poked his head inside. "Goldie, Scream wants to holla at you before he leaves."

"Okay, let me go rap with Scream. Babe, I'll see you at the house." Goldie went to Jordyn and fervently kissed her in front of everyone.

"I never in a million years would've thought y'all two would link up." Whyte said to Jordyn as Goldie left the room. She blushed until she turned a dark pink.

"Hey, man what am I supposed to do with this car. I can't accept that. I'mma police officer." Puncho said to Whyte.

"You think I don't know that. I got everything covered. Surprise, surprise, surprise! All of the paperwork is in order. As far as your gifts are concerned, none of you have anything to worry about." Whyte smiled at Chrissy who had helped him organize this surprise for everyone.

Chapter 21: So What Are We Gonna Do?

"Tonight was the best night of my life. I will never forget it...ever." Money said to Mercedes when he crawled into the bed naked from the waist down.

"Yes, tonight was awesome. I'm so proud of you, I can't even put it into words. Whyte showed out buying everybody new cars. I wonder what you're getting because I know we can't keep the Bugatti." Mercedes was lying in the bed in one of her husband's tank tops. She had decided she was going to talk to him about her breast cancer tonight, or at least before Heavyn came back home from the sleepover this weekend.

"Whatever it is, you can drive it. I just got my new Corvette two months ago. I'm good on cars right now. I hope it's big enough for you and the kids. I noticed you didn't drink any alcohol tonight. I know what that means. When were you gonna tell me?" Money had seen his wife throwing up, barely eating, and sleeping every moment that she wasn't working. He knew she was expecting; he was just waiting for her to tell him.

"Baby, I'm not pregnant. I have breast cancer. The chemotherapy and medicine is what has been making me nauseous and fatigued. That's the reason I have my hair like this; it has started to fall out." Mercedes couldn't even finish her sentence. She burst into tears. She didn't know if she should feel relieved or not. Keeping this from her husband had been one of the hardest things that she'd ever done.

At that moment, Money felt as if the plane he had been riding above the clouds in had crashed. When the words finally penetrated his brain, it seemed like all the air had left his body. The words hung in the atmosphere for a moment. He scooted over closer to his wife, grabbed her tightly, and cried with her. He couldn't contain himself. He was overwhelmed with emotion as he rocked back and forth with his wife who had balled up into the fetal position as she sobbed uncontrollably.

Everything he had accomplished–how far they both had come–was all in vain it seemed. Him selling and breaking down nicks and dimes of crack. Mercedes stealing clothes from Lenox Mall. To him owning the biggest nightclub in Atlanta, and her being a top stylist. None of it mattered when it came to cancer. Cancer was like a bullet. It struck wherever it wanted, no matter what your demographic was.

Mercedes cried until she couldn't cry anymore. She had wanted to be held exactly like this from the day she had received the diagnosis. She needed her husband's strength and assurance. Holding all of this in for so long had been killing her on the inside. Maybe now she could focus her attention on fighting this cancer instead of keeping a secret. She held her head up and looked into the red, bloodshot eyes of her husband. "With us together, nothing can stop us. We didn't survive our childhood in that wild hood, and make it out on top to be taken out by cancer. We're gonna beat this."

"What are we gon' do?" Money said, it was like all his strength had left him and he was once again a small child. His words were uttered softly.

Goldie ended his conversation with D.J. Scream feeling like he had just signed a contract. He couldn't contain his elation. He had to tell someone. He pulled his cell phone out and called Lucky. He knew he was at the studio working. "Man, you are not gon' believe what happened when you left. Okay, first we had a meeting afterwards in the boom-boom room. Whyte bought all of us cars. The Porsche is mine. The Challenger is Puncho's. Everybody else is getting theirs this week. Then Scream sent his assistant in to get me before he left."

Lucky walked out into the hall so he could hear Goldie better. He had become his best friend and knew wherever he went in this music game, he was taking him with him. "Okay, don't hold back on me now big dog. What did D.J. Scream say?"

"He said he had been keeping my CD in rotation since it came out. He played it in King of Diamonds and they went crazy. He sees my potential. He wants to set up a meeting with Rozay. You know what that means don't you Bruh…Maybach Music Group. The hottest in the game right now." Goldie was so excited as he finally left the club.

"Man, bruh it don't get any better than that. That's one of the hottest record labels in the rap world right now. You get in front of Rozay, the sky is the limit." Lucky told Goldie.

"I know man, I know. This has been the best night of my life. That's why when I get home, I'mma go ahead and ask your sister to marry me. I want to be with her forever. I already got the ring and everything. That's the only way I can end this night right here. I'll see you in the morning. I'm heading home to wifey." Goldie ended his call with Lucky after he gave him his blessings on the proposal.

He got into his Yukon. It had been sitting in the parking lot for two days now. He was glad his crazy baby momma hadn't busted the windows. She must not have known it was parked out in the open, or either she was scared to come on club property. Goldie cranked up the Yukon. The bass from the beats that Lucky had been making filled the truck. He lit a blunt that Jordyn had already rolled for him and pulled out of the parking lot.

The light turned red just as he was approaching it. The street was empty. He would have usually run it, but he was vibing off the beats and getting lifted off the kush. A red Range Rover pulled up beside him and two men jumped out. They both were armed with street sweepers that were pointed at him on both sides. The men were dressed in all black with ski masks on. The one on the driver's side yelled for him to get out. Goldie acted like he was reaching for the door. Instead, he mashed the gas pedal and took off.

The masked men began shooting–bullets ripped his truck apart. Goldie tried to duck and drive at the same time. A bullet hit his back tire and sent his truck spinning out of control. It came to rest next to a light pole in the middle of Peachtree Street. He wondered to himself. Where is APD when you need them? His right shoulder was on fire. A bullet had hit him. He looked around for his cell phone but couldn't find it. Just as he reached for his pistol, the doors were snatched open, and he was pulled out forcefully.

Goldie was carried a few feet away to the red Range Rover then pushed inside before the two men joined him. He looked around attempting to make eye contact with the three men in black. He wanted to see if he knew them. Everyone was quiet. Therefore, he couldn't pick up on their mannerisms to identify them. One of their cell phones rang; the man in the passenger seat answered it. "Yeah, we got him. Nope, nobody saw us.

He's in the backseat. He put up a lil' fight. He got hit in the shoulder; he's losing a lot of blood. "What we gon' do?"

Chapter 22: M.I.A.

"I think we need to go away for a while. I have a feeling some shit is about to pop off and I really don't wanna be a part of it." Dude said to Chaney as they got into the car.

Chaney sucked her teeth and rolled her eyes as she glared at her husband. "Well, I'm happy that you're being honest with me now. I don't know what has gotten into you, but keep it up. I hate a liar."

"And I hate a bitch. You ought to be happy that I'm willing to take you with me instead of just getting the hell on." Dude snapped at Chaney. He hated the way she purposely ignored him. Tonight, her silence spoke volumes to him. She didn't even socialize with the other wives. In fact, the only person he saw her speaking to the entire evening was Goldie and Whyte.

"I don't wanna go. I start classes next week. Furthermore, the business is not gonna run itself while you're out getting tans and shopping and shit with your lil' boyfriends. I'll holla at you when you get back." Chaney put her seatbelt on and adjusted herself into a reclining position.

Dude reached over and violently grabbed her by the hair. "When I say jump, you say how high. When I say go, you say where. Don't play with me. I will put your ass right back in the strip club."

"You act like that would be a bad thing. Nigga, I was getting money. I wasn't a nobody. You didn't pick me up from the bus stop. I already had my own condo; I had a luxury ride. I was taking care of my family. I was living nigga. I'm not new to this. You act like you're the second coming. You've been nothing but a bunch of heartache and pain. Nigga, you don't have to send me back. I can pack my shit tonight, leave, and be headlining in a club tomorrow night. Granted, I might have to put up with a lot of bitch niggas, but I won't have to put up with a pussy nigga."

Before Dude knew it, he punched Chaney in her mouth with his fist. When he drew back his fist, it was covered in blood. He looked at her before she folded up into the fetal position and saw that her lip had swollen twice its size in less than three seconds. She screamed loudly. "I'm so sorry baby. Please forgive me. I'm going through so much right now and you're not helping me. You're alienating me even more. Chaney, you hear me? Baby, I'm sorry." Dude pulled away from the club.

Her two front teeth were caught in her lip. When she attempted to pull her lip away from her teeth, blood began to spew everywhere. Her mouth filled with blood. She could care less about how much this car cost as she leaned over and spit a big glob of blood on the floor mat in the front seat. She spit with such force that one of her front teeth came out. Dude had knocked it loose when he punched her.

When Chaney saw her tooth in the blood that she spit out, she went crazy. She started to rain punches on Dude as he drove down the highway. She didn't even feel the pain in her face.

Dude lost control of the car and it left the road.

"Baby, tonight went well in spite of the visit from Dent and his new people. What's that all about?" Chrissy asked Whyte, as she leaned into him while he was unzipping her dress in their master bathroom.

"I really can't say. Me and Jordyn have been enabling Dent for too long. I'mma miss my nigga but he's dead to me now. He's formed an allegiance with the enemy. I reward loyalty and hard work. That's why the team got a fleet of new luxury cars. They received them for staying down and staying true. When he finds out what I got them, he's gon' look stupid."

"He'll find out soon enough. As soon as Pick starts driving that Range everyday, he'll know and start asking questions. All this talk about the enemy, baby you never had enemies as long as you've been in the game. Who is he and what do you know about him?"

"This is business Chris. Let me worry about it. I got it. By the way, did I tell you that you looked absolutely breathtaking tonight?" Whyte turned his wife around to face him. She was dressed in a lace corset, had her heels on, and they were standing eye-to-eye.

"Any enemy of yours is an enemy of mine. We are one. Don't you ever forget that Daviyd!" Chrissy grasped her husband's face and pulled it to hers so he could get her point.

Whyte loved everything about her. The best part was she calmed him. He quieted her down by kissing her firmly and taking her tongue into his mouth. She released a low moan and leaned into him.

"I know I'mma have a hangover tomorrow. Londyn has a football game and you have work. I might need to take a Goody headache powder right now." Tameka said as she sat on their bed taking her shoes off.

"You're gon' have more than a headache. You were going in hard on the Louie baby." Puncho had just stepped out of the shower. He came into the room wrapped in a towel.

"I was drinking for the both of us. You stopped smoking and now you don't drink. You're as straight as an arrow. That's okay, I'll be bad for you." Tameka's voice slurred as she danced naked in front of her husband.

With an instant hard-on underneath the towel, he made his way over to his wife as she danced seductively. Everything that he had discovered wasn't erased from his memory. However, he had forgiven her. As she pulled the towel from around his waist, he kissed her passionately.

She pulled away from the kiss. "Whyte didn't buy you that car because you're his best friend. If that was the case, he would have bought you a car a long damn time ago. Whatever you're doing, please be safe. It's no longer just you. It's the three of us. Please think about us in everything you do." Tameka returned to kissing her husband. She knew something was going on. Tonight only solidified her gut feeling that something in the milk wasn't clean. She paid a price to get her luxury car and knew her husband had paid one for his.

Jordyn struggled to take her dress off. She had been sitting on the bed watching television while waiting for Goldie to come home. He had yet to arrive. She was only five feet; her arms weren't long enough to reach her zipper. She threw herself back on the bed and picked up her phone. One thing she learned being in a clique of niggas is that men hate to be nagged. However, she was worried. She had been home for almost three hours.

The phone went straight to voicemail when she called Goldie. Realizing he was hype about his performance, she thought he may have gone to the studio before he came home. Recently, he had confided in her that going in the studio and recording was a stress-reliever. Also, he said helping her brother set up the studio was one of the best moves he could have made for himself. It appeared that he had stopped frequenting Steady Mobbing all together. Jordyn knew for a fact that he hadn't been there in at least three weeks.

She didn't want to start worrying because when she did, she couldn't stop. Jordyn called her brother, Lucky. He had left the club early, stating some guys had booked studio time so he was heading over there.

Lucky picked up the phone on the first ring. "What's up Jay? What in the world are you doing still awake? It's almost five in the morning."

"I don't have to ask where you are. I can hear the background. Is my hubby over there with you? He hasn't come home yet?" Jordyn told her younger brother.

"Nope, he's not here. About two and a half hours ago, he called me all excited; reporting that Whyte had given him the Porsche and that everyone else was getting cars this week. He mentioned that D.J. Scream had hollered at him and said he wanted to introduce him to Rozay. He was super excited sis. He was leaving the club then. I heard him telling Scream he would hit him up tomorrow. I assumed he was on his way home to you. Let me call and text that nigga. I'mma hit you right back." Lucky could hear the worry in his sister's voice.

Jordyn exhaled loudly as she ended the call with her brother. She didn't care how much this dress cost, she was going to rip it to get out of it. Instead of trying to unzip it, she simply attempted to lift it over her head. Shimmying back and forth, it slowly crept up her body. The sound of stitches ripping was all she heard. She yanked it over her head, went into her closet naked, and came out wearing a Nike bodysuit and some Air Max to match.

After grabbing her purse, keys, gun, and cell phone, she headed out the door. She turned around and glanced at the empty house. Jordyn was filled with apprehension. Something wasn't right. She dialed the one person who always came to her rescue, no matter what. When they picked up, she said, "I'm on my way to pick you up. Goldie's missing."

Chink responded groggily. "Missing, as in M.I.A.? I'll be ready when you get here."

TO BE CONTINUED…

CPSIA information can be obtained
at www.ICGtesting.com
Printed in the USA
LVOW03s2233191217
560318LV00011B/748/P